VULNERABLE

In the Night Trilogy
Book II

Ellen Fritz

Vulnerable

© Copyright 2016, Ellen Fritz
Tell-Tale Publishing Group, LLC
5471 Peri St
Swartz Creek, MI 48473

Cover design by Clarissa Yeo

All rights reserved. No portion of this publication may be reproduced, stored in an electronic system, or transmitted in any form or by any means, electronic, mechanical, photocopy, recording, or otherwise, without the prior permission of Ellen Fritz. Brief quotations may be used in literary reviews.

New Adult Imprint

To my family and friends who constantly encourage me
to keep writing.

Chapter 1

Quinton knew he was being followed.

The gentle footsteps had been with him for over a half mile, stopping when he stopped, speeding up when he quickened his steps, and slowing when he slowed.

It had to be another vampire.

He was sure of it, but the gentle breeze was blowing in Quinton's face and carrying the identifying scent away.

Turning left at the next corner, Quinton kept his pace steady and then turned left again. Now he was going parallel to his previous path. If that vampire insisted on following, Quinton was now downwind and could easily pick up the scent. The breeze at his back would carry the scent right to him.

Quinton had spent many nights searching the streets of Chicago hoping to find any sign of Charles, or anyone who might know where he'd gone. It was a long shot, but odds were that Charles had stayed in Chicago. He was too seriously injured to move very far, and it only made sense that a hidden lair would be fairly close to Nibble.

The Assembly was working every angle they could think of to find Charles, but their fear was that the problem was much bigger than what they'd already uncovered. What if there were other sanctuaries hiding bloodthirst clubs? How many vampires were involved? There were too many questions that had no answers, so their only choice was to start with what they already knew.

The main thing they knew was that Charles had been the head of a sanctuary that catered to those who enjoyed and craved bloodthirst. Eighteen of his followers had already been executed, but none of the Assembly believed that could be all of them. There had to be more hiding somewhere.

Quinton had volunteered to help them look for Charles because he was practically ready to explode with anger and hate. Killing humans was unforgivable and Charles, along with the others that followed him, needed to be stopped.

The sight of those humans Charles held in his basement made Quinton want to rip Charles to shreds, but he'd held back. He'd left Charles alive for the Assembly to question, but that's what had given him the chance to escape.

How many times had he wished he'd just rung Charles's neck as he cringed in pain there on the floor? It would have been so easy. He should have done it, and wanted it to be his hands that found Charles and finally did what had to be done. What should have been done.

Quinton's feelings about what Charles had done to Holly, though, went way beyond hate and anger. Charles and Armand had tried to make her bloodthirsty and God only knew what else he had planned. Holly was the innocent in all this. So young, yet she'd been incredibly brave and strong while facing Charles and Armand, both of them centuries old, powerful monsters.

Seeing her every day while he worked undercover at Nibble had almost driven Quinton crazy. He'd been attracted to her from the beginning, but never made any kind of move on her. She was human when they first met, only seventeen, and needed to be protected from creatures like him.

Even after she was brutally attacked and had to be changed to save her life, it was obvious that she only had eyes for Parker. Parker was the one that made Holly happy. The thing Quinton wanted more than anything was for Holly to be happy.

Quinton still felt guilty for not getting to her sooner that night she was attacked by the bloodthirsty Leslie and Colton. If only he'd been faster, he might have saved her. She might still be a normal human teenager.

But none of Quinton's feelings mattered, because of her feelings for Parker. They were the same age, had been involved before her change, and obviously had deep feelings for each other. Quinton wouldn't do anything to come between them. All he could do for Holly now was take care of destroying Charles.

The re-direction worked and the scent of the vampire wafted to Quinton's sensitive nose, but didn't do him much good. This vampire was a stranger. A stranger that was blatantly following him, and undoubtedly planning his attack. Regardless, the time had come to end this game they were playing.

The road curved sharply, and Quinton ducked into a narrow alley knowing the curve would keep the vampire from seeing where he went. Pressed against the wall, he waited as the footsteps came closer, and still hesitated until the stranger took several steps past him.

Then he attacked.

With a dagger in his right hand, Quinton wrapped his left arm around the vampire's neck. As the muscles of his forearm pressed into his stalker's throat, Quinton levered the head back. He brought the dagger up, and pressed it against the exposed jugular. With a flex of his powerful muscles, Quinton could now snap the vampire's neck or simply slash his throat. What he wanted, though, was answers.

"Why are you following me?"

"I'm not. Just hunting," the vampire gasped. While regular breathing wasn't necessary, a vampire still needed air to talk, and this position wouldn't make talking easy at all.

"On deserted streets?" Quinton said, increasing the pressure of both his arm and the blade against the vampire's neck. He smelled the drop of blood as the knife broke the skin. "Who sent you after me?"

Then all hell broke loose.

Quinton heard the footsteps flying toward him a split second before a sharp pain in his side signaled that he'd been stabbed from behind. Not a killing wound, but enough to cause him to flinch and lose his concentration.

Just as suddenly, two other vampires had each grabbed one of his arms. Quinton felt one of them break the fingers of his right hand, causing the knife to fall to the ground. His left arm was twisted away from the other vampire's throat, and he was held helplessly in place between the two that had sneaked up on him.

The guy that Quinton was ready to torture into giving him some information spun around and began beating him in the face. Now the tables were turned and Quinton knew he would likely die in the next few minutes.

He knew what had happened without needing to even think about it. Was it his stupidity or arrogance that caused him not to see it coming? One vampire had stayed just close enough to be heard and scented while two others followed farther behind. They knew Quinton would find a way to attack.

They had a simple plan to trap him, and he'd fallen for it all the way. With their vampire's speed, they'd gotten him before he could react. He didn't even have time to snap the neck of the guy he once held.

He felt the blood running down his back from the stab wound and over his lips from that last punch that had broken his nose. The next one split his lip and was quickly followed by a hard punch to his gut that made his body want to double over in pain, but the two new vampires were still holding him in place.

Quinton's anger flared more than the pain from the beating and he fought back as much as possible. He tried to twist out of their grips, but they had his arms pinned too tight to get any leverage. He tried to kick out at the one who was doing all the punching, but the others held him against their bodies and he couldn't get the right balance or momentum to kick hard enough to make any difference.

Finally, they must have had enough fun with the punches because they stopped long enough for Quinton to lift his head and look in the hateful eyes of his attacker. That's when Quinton saw the vampire pull a knife from the sheath hidden under his shirt.

The pain of it plunging into his abdomen radiated through his body. That pain was nothing compared to how it felt when that vampire twisted the knife and continued slicing up across his chest, barely missing his heart.

As his blood flowed down his legs and onto the sidewalk, they let him fall. Quinton curled into a fetal position and knew that it wouldn't be long before he lost enough blood that he'd pass out. He also knew that they'd let him suffer through the pain and the certainty of impending death until he was unconscious. Then they'd simply break his neck and finish him.

The last thing Quinton heard was the sound of the three of them laughing as they stood over him. The last thing he saw was a heavy black boot that had been aimed right at his face.

* * *

We'd been able to feel the threat of rain in the air for the last several hours, but were still surprised by the sudden downpour and lashing wind.   We dashed into the closest doorway, which happened to be a Max and Erma's, a place I'd been once before and loved when I was still human and could eat regular food. Now the smell of their famous burgers made me queasy.

Crystal and I were in Columbus at Easton, one of those fancy outdoor malls, and all the regular stores were in the process of closing for the night. The rain wouldn't really have bothered us much if it hadn't been so furious. The paper shopping bags we carried wouldn't protect our newly purchased outfits at all.

So we stood in the entry giving the hostess an apologetic smile because we didn't want a table. We just wanted to wait for the heaviest rain to stop and knew this kind of downpour wouldn't last long.

On my way back from the bathroom where I tied back my rain-soaked hair to get it out of my face, I slipped through the other people who were finding some shelter and saw the back of a big, male vampire talking to Crystal. His scent told me he was a familiar vampire, but someone I couldn't immediately identify, and I figured he'd probably been a client at Rule the Night.

Something about him put me on edge. The expression on Crystal's face, though, bothered me even more. She didn't look angry, or scared, just uncomfortable, questioning. No matter who he was or what he was saying to her, she seemed to be in an awkward situation.

As I approached, Crystal looked at me with the kind of smile that said she was glad to see me. Naturally, the vampire turned to look at what made her smile, and our eyes met. He looked completely flabbergasted and froze for a second. I sneered in the face of one of the vampires I hated most in this world.

Then he turned and dashed for the door like he was scared to death of me. It would have been nice to think he was scared of me, but what really made him run was the reality that I knew him and he'd been discovered.

I grabbed Crystal's arm. "Come on!" I said as I led her through the door to chase him.

"What are you doing?" she gasped as the rain and wind hit us.

I didn't want to lose him, but I knew once he got out of sight of the few humans that were still on the street, he'd turn on his vampire speed and easily get away from us.

"That's Noel!" I shouted as the quickest answer I could give her. Noel had been with Charles at Nibble. Armand was Charles's right-hand-man, but he'd been killed when we rescued the humans that Charles held for bloodthirst. Noel was the head guard and had probably moved into the position right under Charles to replace Armand. It had been Noel that carried Charles out of that basement, enabling him to escape. This guy would know for sure where Charles was and what he was up to. If we could catch him, maybe we could get some answers.

We chased him through two parking lots, across a fairly busy road, and into a patch of woods that was left after construction of the mall. Then he ramped up the speed and left Crystal and me far behind. Vampires got more powerful with age and, even though Crystal was years older than me, we were both just too young to keep up with his top speed.

The other side of the woods was blocked by one of those big walls they build next to freeways to keep some of the noise away from people and to keep people away from the speeding traffic. His scent was scattered and hard to follow because of the rain, but we'd been able to detect it. Then that trace just stopped.

The freeway wall towered over our heads, but there was no doubt that he'd jumped it and kept going across the many lanes and speeding traffic of I270. By this time, he was far gone on the other side, and we'd never be able to find his scent again with all the exhaust spewed out of innumerable cars and trucks.

"We lost him," I sighed.

"Yeah," Crystal sighed back. Then she looked at me instead of continuing to stare at the top of that wall. "But what were we going to do if we caught him?"

"I'm not sure. Maybe get some answers out of him," I said as I wiped rain and stray hair off my face. "I just couldn't let him go."

Crystal nodded, still looking shocked and scared at the thought of facing a powerful vampire like Noel. "Look at us!" she said.

Soaked to the bone, hair plastered to our heads and faces, splatters of mud up our legs, we looked like two drowned rats. I started giggling.

Crystal looked into the soaked shopping bag still clutched in her hand. "We'll have to dry clean our new clothes before we can wear them." Then we both laughed. I think part of that laugh was from relief that we hadn't caught Noel.

Thankfully, our car was in the first parking lot we'd crossed chasing Noel, so we didn't have to go into the main part of the mall again. Of course, with the rain and most of the stores now closed, very few people would have seen us.

I put our bags in the back of the SUV and Crystal got in the driver's seat. We were making a mess of Byron's car, but that wouldn't bother him. The fact that we'd chased someone as dangerous as Noel across Easton would bother him a lot.

"Byron's going to want to skin us alive," Crystal said shaking her head.

"I guess I knew we didn't have any chance of catching him," I said, "but something in me couldn't let him walk away."

Facing Byron after the long drive home, I thought he looked like his head might explode. He was so mad, but really scared, too.

"You chased him into secluded woods where he could have turned and killed you? Did you even consider that he might have been leading you there, away from human eyes, for the sole purpose of killing you? What were you thinking?"

"I was thinking he may lead us to Charles!" Byron had been yelling and I was yelling back. "I couldn't just do nothing!"

"Yes, you could have. And *should* have!"

"No! We have to find Charles, that's the most important thing!"

"Holly," Parker said looking at me like I'd stabbed him in the heart. "How can you say that? Who cares about Charles if something happens to you or Crystal?"

I didn't know what to say because I felt like a complete idiot. I'd chased Noel like he was a naughty puppy and I'd dragged Crystal along with me. Byron was right. He could have easily killed us in those woods. Really thinking about it now, I was surprised he didn't.

"I'm sorry," I finally said quietly. "I guess I wasn't thinking. I just reacted and kept going."

I felt tears building up in my eyes. Why did I always react with tears? Charles getting away after we caught him in Chicago frustrated me beyond belief. The thought of all his killing infuriated me, but those poor humans he kept captive in that cage made me so sad. Not to mention the fact that he was still getting away with his bloodthirst made all of us determined to find him. Now I'd put Crystal in danger and made Parker and Byron so upset. Yeah, I guess I had reason to cry after all.

Byron put his hands on my shoulders. "We know how much you want to stop Charles, but you need to leave that to the Assembly. You're just not powerful enough to deal with him or Noel."

"You're right," I nodded. "I won't take any more chances like that."

Byron squeezed my shoulders, and I looked over at Parker who walked toward me when Byron let go. He hugged me, and a couple more tears slid down my cheek, but then I was able to calm down and get some control.

"Crystal," Byron was saying when Parker and I finally let go of each other. "What did Noel say to you?"

"That was strange. At first I thought he was hitting on me, because he asked if I was staying at the Columbus sanctuary," Crystal told us. "But then he said there was a new sanctuary opening, and was telling me how great it was going to be."

"The Assembly wouldn't establish two sanctuaries in a city the size of Columbus," Byron said.

"That's what I said to him, but he said it was a new kind of sanctuary that was independent from the Assembly. That's when Holly came back."

"An independent sanctuary?" Byron sounded like he was thinking out loud. "I'll notify the Assembly, but I do wonder what he was doing at Easton."

"Not many people were around," I said, "maybe he was hunting."

"Or looking for younger vampires who could possibly be turned to bloodthirst," Byron said.

"Byron!" Luke shouted as he burst through the door. We were in Byron's suite and no one ever threw open his door without knocking, so we all knew this had to be serious. "TJ's taking Quinton to his room!"

What did that mean? Quinton was in Chicago helping the Assembly, wasn't he? We didn't wait to ask. Luke started running down the hall and we followed, getting there just as TJ was laying a big, bloody body on the bed.

"Someone killed Quinton," I whispered to Parker. Not the kind of whisper where you're trying to be quiet, but the kind that results from being so much in shock that only a tiny sound will come out.

Byron was already bending over him, tearing his shirt away from the huge wound in his chest.

"He's started healing," Byron almost sighed. That was really good news. Dead was dead even for vampires. But if there was any life left, our bodies would try to heal us. There was life in Quinton, but he'd need help healing that wound and restoring the blood he'd lost.

"I'll find someone to feed him," TJ said as he turned toward the door.

"What happened?" Byron asked Luke.

"TJ came up to the office to cover the employee entrance, and I was going off duty for the day, when the camera picked up a strange car on the edge of the parking lot. They stopped for a few seconds and drove off. Then we saw some kind of bundle on the ground and called Lorna up to cover us so we could check it out. It was Quinton. Someone dumped him."

Byron thought for a minute before speaking. The only other time I'd seen so much anger and hatred on his face was when we brought the human slaves out of Nibble's basement.

"He was in Chicago looking for Charles," he finally said. "They beat him, bled him, and dumped him on our doorstep. Looks like someone wanted to leave us a message."

None of us had anything to say to that. We knew it was someone working for Charles. We knew he was telling us to leave him alone or suffer the consequences. I hated that they'd done this to Quinton. He was a really sweet guy and helped The Assembly because he believed so deeply that they were right.

"I'd better notify the Assembly while we wait for TJ," Byron said breaking our silence. He didn't go far, just took out his phone as he headed over to the desk. I knew he wasn't about to leave until we knew Quinton had healed enough to gain consciousness.

I had to do something besides staring down at Quinton's bloody body, so I went to the bathroom and soaked a washcloth in warm water to start cleaning the dried blood off his face. I thought I'd feel more confident about him getting better if he didn't look so horrible.

Crystal went somewhere to get a small tub so I could rinse the blood out of the washcloth without going back and forth to the bathroom. Parker and Luke helped us by gently lifting him to get his bloody shirt and pants off, and we started on all the blood covering his chest and legs. We had to change the water in the tub several times.

The gash across his belly and chest was deep and jagged. I couldn't imagine how much that had hurt. The bleeding had stopped, and we could easily see the inside was starting to heal pretty well, but he was way too weak to get better without new blood.

By the time we finished and got him under the covers, Byron was off the phone, and TJ came back with a human donor for Quinton.

The human was older, maybe in his 40's or 50's and looked homeless. Probably an alcoholic who spent his evenings in bars hoping someone would buy him a drink, then spent the rest of the night hiding out or begging. Who knew what he did all day? *My parents probably know him from one of the bars they frequent*, I couldn't help thinking.

He followed TJ in a daze and let himself be led to Quinton's bed. He sat on the edge. The look on his face was empty. TJ had enthralled him, so he had no idea where he was or what he was doing. Once he fed Quinton, he'd be returned to where TJ found him and his memory would be removed. He'd have no idea he took part in any of this.

"TJ and I will handle this," Byron said quietly as he walked over next to the man.

We knew it was time for the rest of us to leave. They would try to get Quinton to bite the man's wrist. If he wasn't able, one of them would do it and drip the blood into Quinton's mouth.

The smell of that human blood was hard for a vampire to resist. Byron and TJ were the oldest and most powerful in the room. The rest of us were too young to be so tempted. I'd resisted that enticing scent in Nibble's basement, but it was the hardest thing I'd ever done. Why take a chance when we didn't have to?

"I'm going up to the kitchen to get that guy some food," Parker said to Crystal, Luke and me as we got out in the hallway.

"He does look hungry," I said sadly. "You want some help?"

Parker smiled. "Thanks, babe, but I'll take care of it."

I'd told him how much human food disgusted vampires. The smell of most of it turned our stomachs, so we avoided the kitchen as much as possible. None of us would have ever thought of feeding the poor guy who was saving Quinton's life. It was too easy to get caught up in our own world and not think about other's needs.

"I wonder what Constance said to Byron," Crystal asked as we sat waiting in the common room.

"What could she say?" Luke answered. "They're in charge because most of us believe in what they stand for and think their rules are the way things should be. Charles is blatantly disagreeing with them by opening an unauthorized sanctuary. They haven't had to fight someone like him for over a century."

"Charles is really powerful, isn't he?" I asked.

"Oh, yeah. And the Assembly was ready to make him a member. Man, they've got to be spooked to know how he fooled them."

"Not to mention a little paranoid," Crystal said. "What if another bloodthirsty one already made it to the Assembly? They have no idea how big this is and can't even be sure if they can completely trust each other."

"That's probably why they wanted Quinton to work for them," Luke added. "He attacked Charles, so he already proved himself."

"You fought against Charles, too," I said.

"But I'm not nearly as powerful as Quinton." Luke smiled. It was simply the truth. "There had to have been several of them to do that to Q."

Parker came back with a bag full of stuff. Peanut butter sandwiches, a hunk of cheese, small cartons of orange juice, three apples, and a package of cookies. "I figured this might last him a couple of days," he said with a shrug.

"It's perfect," I said as I hugged him.

Finally, TJ walked the donor out and told us that Quinton had fed and was resting. Parker gave him the bag of food that he could leave with the guy when he erased his memories. TJ gave Parker a questioning look.

"Just some food. He looks like he hasn't eaten in a while."

"Good idea," TJ shrugged before starting to walk the guy out.

Then we went back in to see Quinton.

Byron sat on the bed next to him and they were talking quietly. Quinton looked a little better, but still didn't look good. He was pale, his cheeks were sunken in and he had dark circles around his eyes. His voice was too weak for us to hear everything he was saying, which means it was really weak since we all had such good hearing. I was sure Parker couldn't hear any sound at all from him.

I reached out to take Quinton's hand and he tried to give me a smile. "You okay?" I asked.

"I will be," Quinton whispered.

"He needs to sleep, and we'll feed him again every several hours," Byron said. We took that to mean it was time for us to leave again to let him rest.

I squeezed his hand. "Don't worry. Byron will take good care of you. Just get better." Somehow he found the strength to smile again.

Chapter 2

Noel saw the back of Charles's hand flying toward him so fast that he had no hope of ducking out of its way. It struck with such force Noel was thrown off his feet and slammed into the cement block wall. Even though Charles was still healing from a broken spine, his power was amazing. That blow would have snapped Noel's neck if Charles had been at full strength.

He felt the blood flowing out of the ear where Charles connected. Then noticed more blood seeping slowing out of the scrape on the other side of his face, where his head had connected with the wall.

Charles stood over him seething. His anger flowed through the room as Randall, another guard that escaped from Nibble, and Clair, a human prostitute, stood silently near the door. They knew better than to draw any attention to themselves when Charles was that angry.

"You had Holly within your grasp and you ran away from her?" Charles growled.

"I'm sorry," Noel said, sounding like he was begging. He didn't dare move from the spot on the floor where he landed. "I was recruiting the other one. I didn't know you wanted Holly back after what she did."

"She betrayed me to the Assembly, got Armand killed, and broke my spine!" Charles roared. His voice echoed through the nearly empty basement. "No one gets away with crossing me, and she destroyed everything I've worked toward for decades! I want to tear her apart with my bare hands. I shouldn't have to tell you that!"

His anger flared again as he kicked Noel in the ribs. Then he kicked him again, and again. Finally, he grabbed him by one leg and spun, slamming Noel head first into the opposite wall.

Charles stood there glaring down at Noel's motionless body. "Do something with him," Charles sneered at Randall. Then he reached out his hand toward Clair.

She walked over, took his hand and followed him down the hall toward his quarters. She knew this wouldn't be a pleasant, gentle feeding, but she'd been there before. Charles had saved her life. Besides, Charles's insane feedings still weren't as bad as the beatings she'd taken from her human pimp.

Once they were gone, Randall cursed under his breath. Charles always left the dirty work to someone else. Resigning himself to being that someone else, he headed out to find a human to give Noel the blood he needed to heal.

Just before dawn, Charles gathered his followers that had escaped from the Assembly at Nibble. Noel was barely coherent after feeding twice, but was strong enough to sit in there and listen. He knew he had to. Charles would have killed him if he'd said he was too weak to attend.

Clair and Randall stood on either side of Charles while Noel sat against the wall. Clair's numerous bite marks and fresh bruises were obvious, but she wouldn't let herself show any discomfort. She knew Charles could have healed those bites, but he got some bizarre power trip by showing them off to his subordinates.

Paul and Deborah were just lucky not to have been in Nibble that night of the attack and their names weren't mentioned to the Assembly. Three others, Clifford, Dawson, and Jeremy, had joined Charles from other parts of the Midwest once he got to Columbus.

His operation in Chicago had been destroyed, but Charles didn't give up easily. He was building again. The hope of joining the Assembly was gone, but that didn't mean all was lost. He was determined to see things go back to the old ways, even if he had to support someone else's rise to prominence.

In fact, a puppet on the Assembly would be safer in the long run. Charles would gladly run the show secretly while others took all the risks of discovery and execution. The problem was finding the right person that was already on the Assembly, yet weak enough to let themselves be used. He'd been working on that and might have recently found the right person.

"Since Noel was too stupid to figure out who my enemies are, I thought I should make it clear to all of you," Charles started. "We wouldn't want anyone else to slip away from us, now would we?" Charles didn't really need to tell his people what would happen if they let another enemy escape. His voice, expression, and past actions did that for him.

"Rule the Night will be destroyed as Nibble was, but I want Byron to see it coming and be powerless to stop it. He and his pathetic followers will not die quickly or easily. I still have some who are loyal to me in Chicago, and they have just finished step one of my plans. Clair is ready to handle step two, and Randall and I will take care of the third step.

"Beyond that, there is only one thing the rest of you need to know. If any of Byron's vampires are spotted, they are to be captured and brought to me. Especially the young one named Holly. I have a very special death planned for her.

"As for recruiting. It seems Noel, in his stupidity, chose the wrong place. Those who lean toward bloodthirst would not be hunting at Easton!" Charles glared at Noel and obviously directed that sentence and his anger toward him. "Get to the seedy parts of town. Find the homeless and the addicts and you'll find bloodthirsty vampires ready to kill them. For now, everyone get plenty of sleep today. We'll be busy tonight."

* * *

Byron had spent most of the night with Quinton and had just come up to let us know that he was healing well. We were all so relieved to hear that.

"I want to talk to you, Holly," he said after the latest report on Quinton. "Would you walk with me?"

"I'd love to," I answered with a smile.

Were Crystal and Parker jealous that I was the one spending the quiet time out on the streets with Byron? No. They both understood. It wasn't about romance, it was about the friendship that started on that rainy night on the elementary school steps. He loved Crystal, and I loved Parker, but Byron and I would always be close. Besides, he was the one that changed me.

"I'm so glad Quinton is healing quickly," I said while breathing in the pleasant spring air.

"He's very strong," Byron answered. "Many would have died from his wounds."

I took his arm and we walked silently for a couple of blocks. The night was clear, cool, and filled with the smell of new growth. Tulips, grape hyacinths, damp earth. It all smelled so fresh and new.

"I talked to your brother, today," Byron said. That was a surprise.

"Is something wrong?" I couldn't imagine why Byron would talk to Chris.

"No," he shook his head. "Well, not dangerously wrong. He's lost his job in that convenience store and had to move back with your parents. He came in to ask me for a job."

"What did you tell him?"

"That I'd get back to him."

"Are you going to give him a job?" Another surprise. How would I feel about Chris working at Rule the Night? That one would take a lot of thought.

"I wanted to ask you, first. You know how busy we've been since everyone's heard about the situation at Nibble. Many look at Rule the Night as a place they know is following Assembly rules. With so many vampires parked in the lot, there's hardly room for the humans. The only available space for more parking is across the street, so I want to start valet parking so customers don't have to travel through the rain and snow. What do you think about me hiring Chris for that?"

"I think it would be great for him, but he doesn't know I'm here." All the secrets. All the lies I'd told him on our infrequent phone calls.

"You'd have to tell him you came back."

"I've been wanting to tell him about Parker," I sighed. "But do you think he'd be safe here? I wouldn't want him used for feeding."

"I think he'd be safe. No one bothers the cooks or Anna, and it'll be almost exclusively human customers that he'll be dealing with. Not many vampires come in just for the evening, but I'll make sure everyone knows he's off limits."

"Byron, I'd love to see him be able to get out of my parent's house." I knew Byron could see the worry and sadness on my face. "I'm afraid they're going to drag him down and get him drinking with them every night."

"Then I'll call him tomorrow," he nodded. "My lease on the lot across the street doesn't start for a couple days, but I'll have him come in to do the paperwork and see how I'm planning on running things. Would you like to see him when he comes in?"

"Yeah," I smiled. "I'd like to surprise him."

I felt a tear roll down my cheek. Why does that happen? I wasn't expecting it at all, and had no clue that it was coming, but there it was, again. And then a second one headed down my face.

"Holly, dear, what's wrong?"

"Nothing," I tried to assure him. "I just realized how much I've been missing him."

"And how much you've worried about him." Byron put his arm around my shoulders.

"That to," I smiled.

"Let's head back," he said. He kept his arm around me and we walked silently back to Rule the Night.

Byron left me at my door and continued down the hall to his suite. I think letting in those feelings of missing Chris, reminded me how much I missed Parker, too. Sure, I saw him every day and we had time to talk and laugh, but that was about it.

I was afraid to hold him and kiss him the way I wanted to. I was afraid to be alone with him because it could tempt us to start something that would encourage that beast inside me. And he was being so patient, so understanding. He said he'd wait forever if necessary and that was what he was doing.

I loved him so much and wanted nothing more than to be with him. Before I knew what I planned on doing, I walked out of my room and down the hall to Parker's room where I knew he was sound asleep. I needed so much to be close to him.

I stood outside his door and listened to his quiet, gentle breathing. Every so often, there was a little sound that I thought would probably turn into a snore when he got older. No, he'd be a vampire once he graduated and never get older than he was right now. I closed my eyes and longed for that day when Byron would change him.

The knob turned easily. He really should be locking his door with all the unfamiliar vampires staying here these days, but he often forgot. I'd remind him again. I walked in as silently as only a vampire can and closed the door behind me.

Standing next to his bed, I watched him sleep. So peaceful. So handsome. So sexy. I breathed in his warm, familiar scent and wanted nothing more than to climb in next to him. Instead, I just stood there.

My emotions were all over the place. I felt love, desire, and a nagging loneliness. How could I be lonely when surrounded by all those who I cared about, and those who cared about me? I guess I was lonely for the love Parker and I could share if I was strong enough.

I'd had so much strength in that horrible basement at Nibble. Why couldn't I have that kind of control with Parker? Something about his blood tempted me like nothing else. His scent somehow connected with that part of me that wanted to drink until there was nothing left. The part I called the beast.

When I was learning to control myself, I told Byron that the hunger was like an addiction. I'd overcome that addiction and had complete control when feeding. Except with Parker.

His blood was different. The scent of his blood could make the beast battle his way through all my defenses. If the beast got out, I would devour him.

I shouldn't have been standing there thinking about his blood. That was just stupid. I realized I was listening to his heart and feeling the rush of his blood through his body.

My fangs started to descend and I licked my lips remembering the taste. The enticing taste of Parker's blood. I remembered it so well from when I almost drained him, and my beast wanted to taste it again.

I crossed my arms against my chest like I was physically holding myself back and mentally pushed on that beast that was trying to find its way out. Then I ran from his room. As I started to close the door, I found the determination to turn that little knob that would lock his door behind me. I didn't need the temptation of knowing I could easily go back to him.

I sat on the floor leaning against my bed, barely remembering the dash back to my own room. My knees were up to my chest with my arms crossed on top of them and my forehead rested on my arms. Why was Parker's blood my greatest temptation? Was it because I loved him so much, or had his blood caused me to love him? I didn't know.

I did know I couldn't ever do that again. I had to make myself stay away from being alone with him. I knew it was the beast that had led me to his room and made me think about tasting him. Never again. *Game on, beast*, I thought. *You will not win this battle.*

I hardly slept that day and couldn't resist calling Parker as soon as he got home from school. We met in the empty bar because he was hungry and wanted to get a sandwich from the kitchen. He usually ate his dinner later when Beth and Abe, the human cooks, came in to make bar food for the human customers.

He brought out a plain cheese sandwich, a glass of milk, and a banana. None of those were smells that especially bothered me, so it wasn't hard to sit with him while he ate. He probably chose those foods on purpose because he knew they wouldn't bother me as much as the left-over lasagna that I knew was in the fridge.

"So Chris is coming in to talk to Byron today?" he asked after I'd told him about Byron giving him a job.

"Yeah. Probably pretty soon."

"I'd like to meet him, if it's okay with you."

"I forgot you've never met him," I smiled. Amazing that the two most important guys in my life had never met. "I'd love it. I'm going to tell him that I came back to Adelle to be with you, so he'll definitely want to meet you."

"He'll think we're living together." Parker gave me a look asking if that was all right.

"I know, but that's okay. Besides, we're engaged," I smiled.

"Yeah," he sighed, reaching over to take my hand. Then he snorted a little laugh. "It still amazes me that you said yes. I was so scared to ask you."

"How could I resist saying yes to the man I love?"

He pulled my hand toward him, kissed my palm, and held my hand against his cheek. "I love you so much, Holly."

"Me, too."

"Ah-hum," I heard behind us. "Don't mean to interrupt," TJ said while trying to keep from smiling, "but Byron wanted me to tell you that Chris will be here in about a half hour."

"Tell him we'll wait in the common area until he calls, okay?" I answered.

"Sure thing. See you later."

"Not much for anyone to interrupt between the two of us," Parker sighed as we headed downstairs. "But wait until my change." He waggled his eyebrows in a know-what-I-mean kind of look. I giggled like a twelve year old. I hate when I do that.

It seemed no time at all before Byron called.

"Did you tell him I'm here?" I asked.

"No, I thought you wanted a surprise."

"Good, we'll be right there." My smile was huge. "Let's go," I said to Parker.

I opened the door to Byron's office and saw Chris's back as he sat in a chair across from Byron's desk. His head was bent while he wrote something. My smile had gone from huge to taking over my whole face.

"Hey, Chris," I said quietly.

He spun around, leaped out of the chair, and had his arms around me before I knew what was happening. It seemed like he moved with vampire speed. "Holly!" was all he said.

"I missed you, too!" I said as we hugged and he lifted me off my feet.

"What're you doing here?" His expression was a mix of confusion and joy.

"I live here, now." Then I told him a story about Parker and me getting involved when I worked here, how we stayed in touch while I was gone, me coming back to be with him, and us getting engaged. Some of it truth, most of it lies.

"This is Parker," I finally said as I moved away from Chris.

"Hi, Chris," Parker said reaching out his hand.

"Hey, man," Chris answered as they shook. "I can't believe this," he looked back at me smiling. Then he got a more serious look. "You look great, Holly. Like you're really happy."

"I am." My smile was huge and I knew Chris had no doubt I was telling him the truth. "And now we'll be able to see each other every day."

"I'm sorry about the phone," he sighed. "I just couldn't pay for it anymore."

"I understand," I smiled and nodded.

"That reminds me, Chris," Byron said opening his desk drawer. "You'll need this to keep in touch with the front door guard." He tossed Chris a phone.

"Thanks." The look on his face was priceless.

Byron told him to show up at 6:00 the next evening, and we walked out to the bar.

"We'll have plenty of time to get to know each other," Parker said, touching Chris on the shoulder. "I'll let you talk to Holly."

With that Parker headed for the back hallway, and Chris and I sat down to talk. He said nothing had changed with Mom, Dad or Uncle Steve, but I did appreciate knowing they were okay. At least as okay as usual.

Chris had been staying in my old room since he lost his apartment a few weeks before and had been looking everywhere for a job. He remembered me telling him that I worked at a place called Rule the Night and thought he'd give it a shot.

"When Byron said he'd get back to me, I really thought he was just giving me the brush off, you know?" Chris told me. "I was blown away in there when he told me about the valet parking. He's putting me in charge and paying me more than I ever figured he would. I'll be able to get my own place in a few weeks."

"I have some money saved if you need it for a security deposit or anything. Maybe you could move out sooner."

"Thanks, but I think it'll be okay at Mom and Dad's until I get things together, but I won't tell them how much I'm making. They'll want rent."

"Yeah, they will," I sneered. They couldn't pass up the opportunity to have extra cash around.

"I just can't believe I start a good job tomorrow," Chris sighed, shaking his head.

"It'll be great," I smiled.

Inside my head, I knew too well how dangerous this job could be and how many secrets there were at Rule the Night. Especially the secret that Chris's little sister wasn't human anymore.

Chapter 3

The next few weeks went by very quietly and uneventfully. After the time I'd had in Chicago, quiet and uneventful was exactly what I needed. We all needed it.

Chris settled into his new job and got a lead on an apartment that should be available by the end of the month. Quinton healed completely and went back to guard duty even though he expected the Assembly might call him back to work for them at any time.

Before I knew it, it was April and Parker's birthday was coming up. Byron was giving him a suite, and the rest of us were decorating it, so it would be a gift from all of us.

Sounds good, but I racked my brain trying to think of something special from me. I went round and round and still couldn't think of anything that was meaningful enough. I certainly didn't want to get him some lame table or something.

Everyone knew it was just a matter of weeks before Parker would graduate. Byron would change him, and that suite would be a home for Parker and me. That was the most important thing, when Parker and I could start our lives together.

Still, I wanted my gift to be something that would be for him, but also about the two of us. So Crystal and I shopped.

We went everywhere from cute antique shops to IKEA, but nothing I'd seen was right or special enough. I was starting to think I'd never come up with anything, so I tried to put it out of my mind by going with Crystal to look at couches.

She took pictures of several different ones to show Byron. Watching her with the digital camera, I suddenly had a brainstorm. Crystal always took pictures, and I knew she had several of Parker and me saved on her little data stick, but there was one in particular that I was remembering.

"Crystal, remember the picture you took of Parker and me in front of Byron's fireplace?" I asked.

"Which one? I think I have several."

"The one where we're holding hands and looking at each other. Do you still have that one?"

She fiddled with the camera and scrolled through dozens before coming to the one I was remembering. There it was. Parker and I had both our hands clasped, leaning slightly away from each other like we were going around in a circle, and staring into each other's eyes.

It was the look that made it special. We gazed at each other with so much love, that it seemed there was no one else in the world but the two of us. At the time, we had no idea anyone was taking pictures, and I was a little embarrassed when I first saw it.

"That's such a sweet picture," Crystal said.

"It's more than that," I sighed. "Parker's favorite picture is one of himself with his parents. It's the same pose, but it's the look on their faces that means so much to him. We have the same look."

Crystal's eyes got sparkly, holding back a tear. "It's how much you love each other," she whispered.

"Yeah," I answered with a huge smile. "I want to get it enlarged and framed."

"Oh, Holly, that's so romantic. And, you know what? I don't think Parker's ever seen it."

"Really?"

"Remember? I showed it to you one night in the bar. I don't think I ever got around to showing this group to Parker at all."

"That's so perfect. He'll love it." I couldn't stop looking at it and knew that Parker would have a hard time taking his eyes off it, too.

"We'd better get to the frame shop so they have time to get it done."

A few days later, I dragged Parker to his birthday celebration in Byron's suite where we usually met for occasions. I noticed the funny look on Parker's face when he looked around and noticed there were no gifts or anything, just the employees sitting around chatting. He was going to be so surprised!

The cooks brought in a cake with a big 18 piped on the top and all the candles lit. Parker blew them out easily, and he cut pieces for himself, Sarita and Anna, the only humans in the room. Maybe I'd take a piece to Chris when he got to work later. He didn't know about vampires so couldn't be included even though I would have loved to see him at this party.

I told Beth and Abe what a good job they'd done and felt bad, as usual, that I didn't know them very well. They were a human couple that I rarely saw because they were always in the kitchen, and none of us vampires ever wanted to go in there. The constant smell of greasy, spicy bar food that filled that kitchen was something we all avoided.

"Well, Parker," Byron said once the cake was eaten. "Time for a birthday present. Come over here."

"Going to bite me?" Parker asked with a grin, tilting his head to one side, exposing his neck.

"Stop it," Byron said trying to look stern and angry, but he couldn't keep the smile from his eyes.

When Parker got to him, Byron turned him around and put a blindfold over his eyes. "Let's go," he said as he put a hand on each of Parker's shoulders and started to lead him out. Parker didn't say anything, but I could see his furrowed brows above the blindfold that showed his brain was working frantically to figure out what was up.

We paraded Parker down the hallway. I scooted ahead to open the door to the new suite, and Byron led him right in. Everyone else ducked in around them and found seats. Then Byron took off the blindfold.

I laughed at the expression on Parker's face. It started out with confusion and curiosity, then changed to revelation as he realized this new place was his gift.

"This is mine?" he gasped.

"From all of us," Byron said as he swept his arm around the room indicating the friends that surrounded Parker. "Everyone had a hand in the decorating and finishing. Maybe Holly should give you a tour."

I took his hand as he turned and looked at the room. We'd put together an eclectic mix of old and new from an antique, mahogany buffet to the sleek, modern couch and chairs. It all went together in earth-tone colors and made the space feel comfortable and homey.

Parker smiled and hugged me. He whispered in my ear, "It'll be *our* home." I almost cried.

I walked him through a small office/den that connected the living room and bedroom. I could see him some day doing office work for Byron and playing the video games he couldn't resist. Then we stepped into the bedroom.

He took one look at the king-sized bed and wiggled his eyebrows at me before kissing my cheek. Yeah, we could both picture ourselves sharing that bed. Then I turned him around to the built-in shelves that filled one wall. They were mostly empty now but would hold books and knick-knacks when everything was moved from his old room.

Next to the shelves, though, was the picture I wanted him to notice. Framed to match the woodwork was an 11x14 print of the picture Crystal had taken. It had turned out even better than I'd expected and I loved it. Hopefully, Parker would, too.

He looked at it, looked back at me, and stared back at it again. His bottom lip trembled a little and I knew he saw what I'd seen in that picture. Then he couldn't hold it in and a tear slid down his face as he turned back to take me in his arms.

He held me so tight I thought he'd never let go. Finally he moved back a little and took my face in his hands so we were staring at each other.

"How can I ever explain how much that means to me?"

"You don't need to explain."

"Yeah, I do. I don't like to think about it, but losing my parents left a huge hole in me. I love Byron, but that hole's still been there. You fill it, Holly. That look in your eyes. In the picture and what I'm seeing right now. You fill it. That's all I'll ever need."

The tears were rolling down my cheeks, and there was nothing I could say. I gently kissed his lips and we held each other again.

When I opened my eyes I saw Byron peeking through the open door. I had forgotten that everyone was still in the other room. Obviously, Byron wanted to give us a minute, but there was a party going on.

"We should go back out," I said quietly.

"Or never leave this room again," Parker smiled.

He took my hand and we went back out to the friends and family gathered for his birthday party.

* * *

Chris reported in at the guard's office every night before he headed back outside to start parking customers' cars. He always wore a black jacket that said VALET across the back and had *Rule the Night* written in script on the left of his chest. I often smiled when I saw him because he looked so official. Byron had said he was doing a great job. I was proud of him.

"Want some cake?" I asked as I met him at the office door. He was talking to Luke. They seemed to get along really well and were getting to be friends. If the parking got really busy, it was Luke that went out to give Chris a hand.

"Yumm ... can't resist cake," Chris smiled.

"You have time to sit in the bar?"

"Enough time to eat this."

We both loved being able to see each other every day. As kids we'd played together all the time with the same group of neighborhood friends. Then we went through the teenage years when we each had to look out for ourselves because Mom and Dad were so hard to deal with. Then Chris moved out, leaving me on my own. Now, we were together again.

"Hey ..." Chris said after he'd swallowed three big bites of cake. "Uh ... I wanted to see you tonight. Mom's in jail again."

"Who'd she hit this time? Dad or, hopefully, Uncle Steve?"

"Neither. It was a cop outside of Chips."

"You're kidding! How drunk was she to hit a cop?" Even Mom and Dad usually had more sense than that.

"Pretty damn drunk," Chris frowned as he took his eyes off the cake and looked up at me. "Dad says it's really serious this time. Besides hitting a cop, it's her third arrest. She could get 90 to 120 days."

"In jail? She could be in jail for three or four months?"

"Yup. No more time served or long weekends."

"Damn! As mad as I get at her, I never wanted to see her in jail. But, I don't know, maybe it's what she needs."

"It'll get her sober," Chris frowned.

"Yeah," I nodded.

"I thought the same thing."

"I worry about them," I said quietly. "I've worried about you, too. Living with them again can't be fun."

Chris let out one of those half-laugh/half-snort sounds. "No … it's not fun at all. That's why I came here. I was getting desperate to find something. I have to get out of there."

"I know the feeling."

"Holly, I was starting to drink with them every night. I know I can't let myself do that, but I can't just turn my back on them, either," he frowned and shrugged. "They're the only parents we have, you know? I guess they're better than none at all."

"Parker's parents were killed. That's when Byron adopted him. I've thought about that a lot."

"I didn't know that. Does make you think, huh?"

"Sure does. Do you think I should call Dad and let him know I'm back in town?"

"That's up to you, little sis. I haven't told them."

"I'll think about it. Let me know what happens with Mom, okay?"

"Sure, but I'd better get to work before I get fired," he winked.

Chapter 4

Since the whole episode with Charles (I couldn't bear to think about it as the episode that started when I tried to drain Parker), things had changed around Rule the Night. We had more clients and customers, more guards because we were all much more careful about strangers, and I had Chris in my life again.

With all the new business, Luke started helping Crystal and me at the bar most nights when he wasn't helping Chris. The guards sent by the Assembly were mostly off the streets since there'd been no sign of any bloodthirsty or unknown vampires, so they took over the regular guard duties, and Luke enjoyed going back to bartending.

Luke still had a lot of fun flirting with the customers, but he'd cooled it on the disgusting stuff. He was friendly, funny, and made all the girls smile. I guess it *was* all an act at Nibble like Quinton said. Whatever, I liked this new Luke a lot better.

The change I loved the most, though, was that Parker was up in the bar most evenings. Byron had always kept him out because he was afraid someone would want to feed from him. Well, that wasn't as much of an issue now since all the vampires could easily see that Parker was with me.

He always sat at the end of the bar, and I sauntered over to him whenever I wasn't with a customer. The way we held hands and talked quietly made it obvious that Parker was one human not available to feed other vampires because he was feeding me. Of course he wasn't feeding me, but it was mighty convenient to let the vampire clients think he was.

But having Parker in the bar could be a problem, too. One night he came up from his room while I was flirting with a guy to feed. I didn't even see him there, but he watched the whole thing.

Parker wasn't mad because he knew I had to feed, but I think he was hurt. It had to hurt him a lot to watch me pick up a strange guy and take him to one of those private rooms.

When I came back to the bar, Crystal told me what he'd seen and that he'd just left to go back to his suite. I tried to talk to Parker, but he kept saying that it was cool, no problem. I let the subject drop. I knew he wanted to feed me and hated that I had to go to strangers, but felt like I needed to reassure him.

I ended up telling him I loved him and paying a lot more attention to him when he was in the bar. After that night, I was more careful and made sure Parker wasn't around when I fed.

Byron came in before closing like he usually did, sat at the end of the bar next to Parker, and signaled Luke, Crystal, and me to join them. I wondered what this was about.

"You two remember Clair from Nibble?" he asked Luke and me.

"One of the girls upstairs," Luke said. "The one I fed from after Noel jumped me."

"That's about all I know about her," I said. "I hardly ever saw her in the bar."

"She didn't come down much," Luke added. "I think Charles kept her for himself most of the time." The look on his face told us it couldn't have been pleasant for her.

"Well, she came in tonight to ask about working here," Byron said.

"Didn't the Assembly settle her somewhere?" I asked.

"She says she can't make it on her own and can't find any work in Chicago. She offered to start feeding vampires again. I explained we don't operate like Nibble."

"I think Charles treated her pretty rough," Luke said quietly. "She went from a sleazy pimp to a sleazier vampire," he shook his head. "Can you help her?"

"I'm starting her tomorrow night as a waitress, but she worries me. She was under Charles's influence for a long time, so we'll all have to watch her."

"We will," I said.

"Thanks," Byron smiled.

"So, will clients be allowed to feed from her?" Parker asked.

"Sure, like any human in here. Except you," Byron gave him a fake mean look. Parker smiled at him. "And I told her she could let the vampires know she's aware of what's going on if they approach her. The thing is, it'll be her choice and can't get paid for anything. She didn't have a choice at Nibble."

"That sounds good," Luke added. "It'll be so much better for her here."

"I have another concern, though, and I'm not sure of a solution," Byron continued. "Crystal and I have talked about it, but she's not sure either. It's Chris, Holly. He's the only human employee that doesn't know about us. He's out there alone every night and wouldn't even recognize a threat until it was too late. I'm not ready to tell him, yet. Besides, even if he knew, I don't know how he'd recognize a vampire among the humans."

"I could work with him," Parker said. "I pretty much just hang around every night so I wouldn't mind giving him a hand. Even though I'd miss Holly," he smiled at me.

"That's not a bad idea," Byron said, "but you still wouldn't be able to distinguish whether someone is a vampire or not."

"Sure, I can. As long as I'm close enough to smell them."

"Smell them?" Byron's eyebrows went up and I think he looked a little offended. The rest of us had the same expressions.

"Are you saying we smell?" I asked.

"Well, yeah ... not bad, or anything, but you have a distinctive smell. Actually, I like the way vampires smell."

Luke started laughing first, but the rest of us joined right in. "What do we smell like?" he asked through his snickering.

"Don't you guys smell it?" Parker looked amazed at the way this conversation was going. I couldn't blame him for that.

"We smell individuals," Byron explained. He was trying to be serious, but couldn't keep the grin off his face. "Are you saying we all smell alike to you?"

"Yeah. Except Holly. I recognize her scent, but I've been closer to her than to any of the rest of you," Parker shrugged and grinned at me.

"I still want to know what we smell like!" Luke said while grabbing Parker's shoulder and shaking it, and still laughing.

"Okay, okay. It reminds me of the fall. You know, like when the leaves cover the ground and you can smell them in the air. The whole downstairs kinda smells like fall."

"We smell like dead, decaying leaves?" Luke said trying to look offended. He still looked like he was laughing hysterically inside.

"But not in a bad way," Parker smiled. "You smell kinda warm and earthy."

"Mmmm ... earthy. I guess that's better than dead leaves," Luke said and started laughing out loud again.

"How long have you been smelling us?" Byron asked more seriously. I think he was too curious to keep laughing. The concept that Parker could smell us was something he never considered.

"Since I got here. But I guess it took about a year before I realized it was the vampires I was smelling."

"Good heavens," Byron sighed. "So humans can smell us, they just don't know what they're smelling."

"I do," Parker said with a fake, proud grin.

We all started laughing again.

"Then I'll tell Chris you'll start working for him tomorrow night," Byron said. "If you *smell* any potential problems, you can call the guards."

"I work *for* him?"

"Yes you do," Byron said more seriously. "I put him in charge of the valet service, so he's your boss. Doesn't matter who your dad is."

I smiled. Chris was so going to love being someone's boss. He'd had too many crappy jobs in his past and Parker had never had a job at all. It might be pretty interesting to see how this worked out.

* * *

Chris smiled and tried to pay attention to the couple he was helping out of their car, but couldn't help watching Lorna as she stood at the door to the bar. She scowled at everyone while waiting for an ID that proved they were over 21. And that was her pleasant face for the customers who were legal. If someone tried to get in when they were under 21, or by carrying a fake ID, her look turned deadly.

Her brows furrowed, her eyes narrowed and her mouth sneered. Chris had to smile to himself. He'd seen the big, green eyes that tilted slightly at the ends, flash with laughter. The lips she used to sneer so menacingly were full, wide, and could produce a smile to melt a man's heart.

Chris knew she had to be about 5' 11", because he could stare right into those sparkling eyes while talking to her, and he was an even 6' tall. The short, jagged cut, dark hair that framed her face made her look like a pixie when she smiled, but then like a bad-ass when she was on door duty.

Lorna wore the same uniform as the other guards – black jeans and a black t-shirt with *Rule the Night* written over her left breast and GUARD written across the back, but she sure didn't look like the other guards. The slim-cut jeans showed how her legs went on forever and ended in the hottest butt Chris had ever seen. The shirt hugged her just enough to show off a body that was incredibly feminine, yet amazingly muscular.

He couldn't wait until closing when they'd have a minute to talk. He wanted to ask her out so bad, but had just been too intimidated. Not by her strength and training, even though he'd seen her face down guys a lot bigger than her and she always won. He was intimidated because she was so gorgeous.

Why would someone like her want to go out with someone like Chris? Yeah, girls had always said he was handsome and hot, but he had nothing. This was the best job he could have hoped for, was just moving out of his parents' house, and didn't even have a high school diploma. The only things he owned were the clothes that Gretchen had bought him. Hell, it'd probably be a year before he could afford a car, even a really old used one.

But she did give him plenty of those smiles that melted him when no customers were around. She seemed to enjoy their chats and she laughed at his jokes. That was all at work, though. Didn't mean she wanted to spend any other time with him.

Finally, it was 1:45. Only two cars were left in the lot across the street, Parker had left to retrieve one of them, and Chris stood at the door with Lorna. Two customers left, walked in opposite directions down the street, and they were alone.

"Busy night," Lorna said. "You heading right home to get some sleep?"

From any other girl, Chris would have taken that as an opening, but, man, he just didn't know. "I'm never sleepy right after work," he said. "It'll be a couple hours of TV before I hit the pillow."

She smiled. "Me too. I usually don't feel sleepy until dawn."

Okay, it's now or never. She might turn him down, but then he'd at least know. "You wanna' go get something to eat?"

"Is there someplace open at this hour?"

Chris's heart started beating a little faster. That wasn't a no. "The diner on 3rd Street is open all night."

"I'm really not hungry, but it'd be nice to sit and talk for a while."

"Yeah, we never get to say more than two words out here with the customers."

"Why don't we meet in the guard's office after we both check out?"

"Great! Parker's bringing over one of the cars left in the lot, I'll go get the other one, and meet you later."

"See you then, Chris."

Chris's stomach clenched a little as she gave him one of those smiles. He smiled back and dashed across the street as Parker was pulling a car up to the curb. Chris felt like his feet hardly touched the ground 'cause he couldn't believe the beautiful, incredible Lorna was actually going out with him.

"What's got him moving so fast?" Parker asked as he got out of the car he'd just parked at the front door.

"We're going out when we're off duty," Lorna smiled.

"You know he's off limits."

"Of course I know that! We're just going to a diner to talk." Lorna's grin said exactly what she was thinking.

"You like him!" Parker was surprised and didn't try to hide it.

"I think he's sweet as can be, and hot as hell," she smiled.

Parker saw her gaze across the street and knew that her vampire vision enabled her to see him from where they stood. "You're watching him, aren't you?"

"Can't blame a girl for looking," she winked.

Parker laughed. "Holly and I thought it would be you and Luke."

"Luke's nice, but Chris has something else. Something special."

"Believe me, I get it. His sister has something special, too. But, be careful, Lorna. Byron and Holly will both go ballistic if you feed from him."

"Don't worry. I fed last night and I have no intentions of turning Chris into a snack. He'll just be pleasant company for the rest of the night."

A customer came out and claimed the car Parker had brought to the curb. Chris pulled up with the last car for the night.

"Hey, Parker," Chris smiled. "You can go ahead and call it a night. This is the last one."

"Thanks. Working 'till closing makes Friday's pretty long."

"How long 'till graduation?"

"Only a few weeks, and I can't wait." Everyone, except Chris, knew that Byron would be changing Chris right after graduation which meant he and Holly could be together.

It also meant that Parker'd have to stay away from Chris until he had control of his instinct to feed. That's when they'd probably have to tell Chris the truth of what Rule the Night was and that his little sister and new friends were vampires.

Chris smiled. "Go get some sleep."

"See you guys tomorrow."

The last customer came out as Parker was going in, and Chris headed over to the car to open the door for him. Lorna gave him a big smile, went through the front door, and locked it behind her. Chris couldn't wipe the smile off his face as he watched those long legs disappear behind the door. He ran around the building to go in the employee entrance and meet Lorna inside.

Walking slowly next to each other, they crossed the side parking lot and started down the sidewalk. Chris stopped walking as he started to feel a little embarrassed.

"Lorna," he said, "I never told you the diner is almost a mile away. I mean … you've been on your feet all night. You sure you want to go?"

"Of course! I'm not tired. And I love walking in the dark on a beautiful spring night. Especially with a good looking guy," she smiled.

Chris felt like he was melting. "I just wish I had a car to drive you."

"That doesn't matter. Besides, Byron has six cars sitting in that garage, and he'd let us use one any time." She smiled and took his hand. "This is perfect."

Chris squeezed her hand and started walking again. He didn't say anything because he was now too melted to speak. This was the most amazing woman he'd ever met. If she never spoke to him again, the smile she gave him as she grasped his hand would be a great memory for a lifetime.

They were soon sitting across from each other sharing the diner with a guy at the bar who was trying to drink enough coffee to sober up, and another couple about five booths away. It wasn't the nicest or cleanest place, but at least it was quiet.

"You sure you don't want anything?" Chris asked.

"I'm sure, but you go ahead and get something," Lorna said. Inside her head she was begging him not to get anything too greasy or smelly. The mixed scents in the diner were already giving her stomach problems. But she wasn't going to control him. She was determined to play this like they were both human.

"I'm good," he said. He'd ordered a Mountain Dew, but she'd only gotten water. He sure hoped that wasn't because she thought he couldn't afford to buy her something.

"So, Chris, what do you like to do when you're not working?"

"I don't have hobbies, or anything, but I joined a boxing club a couple months ago. I go there most evenings before work."

"You look like you enjoy it."

"Yeah," Chris smiled with a thoughtful look. "A lot of people think it's just brutal, but it's not. It's more about control and timing. You have to think and analyze your opponent. You're always judging how and when to strike. It's a lot more than I thought it was going to be."

"You describe it well," Lorna nodded. "I used to box, and I know it can be an intense workout."

"Watching you handle some of those guys outside the bar, I'm not surprised at all that you boxed. You are one strong woman."

"Yeah, I can take care of myself," she grinned. "Tell me about some of your matches."

Chris usually didn't like talking about himself much, but Lorna made it easy. Besides, while she listened, she had a habit of opening her lips slightly and stroking her tongue over her top teeth.

He only caught glimpses of it. I was so sexy, he had a tough time keeping his eyes off her mouth while he talked, and he didn't think she had any idea she was doing it.

"Where do you live?" Chris asked as they left the diner about 4:30. "I'll walk you home."

"At Rule the Night," Lorna answered as if she assumed he knew that.

"Oh. I knew Byron lived there with Crystal … and Holly and Parker, of course, but I didn't know anyone else did."

"The guards. It makes it easier with all the different shifts and stuff." Lorna hadn't thought about how little Chris knew about Rule the Night. There were a lot of secrets, and she wondered how long Byron could keep everything from him.

"That makes sense," he said. His expression, though, said he had a lot of questions.

"So why don't I walk you home?" Lorna grinned.

"No! I couldn't leave you to walk back to the bar alone."

"I think we've crossed that threshold where all the stalkers have gone home and the only people out are the early-morning joggers."

"You're probably right, but I can't leave you alone out here."

"Okay," she said.

They stood at the bottom of the steps outside the employee entrance. "I had a good time," Chris said.

"Yeah, it was nice."

"Maybe we could have dinner before work sometime?" he asked.

"We'll have to look at my schedule. I'm on the employee door a lot of afternoons."

"You work some long hours."

"Sometimes," she shrugged.

As they talked Chris realized they'd both moved a little closer to each other, and Lorna was doing that little tongue-to-teeth thing again. He had to kiss this amazing woman. He raised his hand to her cheek and leaned in to her lips.

The kiss stayed gentle for several seconds, but then her arms were around him and her hands were stretched out across his back. He couldn't believe how much strength he felt in her as their bodies pressed together. It felt incredible. He stroked her cheek with his thumb while his other hand spread through her hair and held the back of her head.

Their lips separated slightly and Lorna whispered, "You taste wonderful," as she moved her hand to the back of his head and tipped it to the side. Then her lips were on his neck. It was like electricity shot through his body. He moved to nuzzle her ear and she sighed deeply against his neck.

Lorna suddenly pulled away from him. "I forgot … we're on camera here."

"Oh, shit!" Chris said, and backed away.

"Maybe I should have walked you home," she smiled.

"Do you think anyone's watching?"

"Oh, yeah! I think TJ's called Quinton and Luke over to share the laugh."

"You think they'd be mad if I flipped them off?"

Lorna laughed. "Luke would love it."

"Come here," Chris said as he took her hand and led her to the edge of the front sidewalk where the camera lens couldn't reach.

He took her face in both his hands and kissed her again. She had her hands on his chest, right over his heart.

"You going to send me in there to face them alone, aren't you?" she teased.

"It's that or go home with me, but I won't expose you to the assholes that pass as my father and uncle. Once I have my own place, we'll talk."

"Yeah. We'll talk," she smiled and he melted again.

"Damn, Lorna," he whispered. "I think I need to leave. See you tomorrow."

"I look forward to it."

Chris let go of her and walked away backwards so he could keep looking at her. She gave him a killer smile and blew him a kiss. He turned and jogged toward home, but he could still feel her pressed against him and still feel her lips.

If they'd had a place to go, he knew they'd have been all over each other. But it was better this way. Lorna was too wonderful to be a one-night-stand after what was barely a date.

He'd find a way to take her someplace nice. If she wanted to come back to his new place, he'd gladly welcome her in his bed, and in his life. Chris shook is head in amazement realizing that she could be someone he wanted to be with for a long time.

Lorna walked through the employee door when TJ opened it and she glared at him. She'd been right. Quinton and Luke were there, too.

"Say one word or crack one smile and all three of you will be healing for days."

"You feeling okay, Lorna? You look a little flushed," Luke said with fake concern on his face.

Lorna grabbed him by the throat with one hand as he fought to suppress his laughter. "You, I could break in half!" she sneered. Then she started smiling as the laugh broke through Luke's lips. She heard the chuckles from TJ and Quinton behind her.

"Get your own humans!" she spat out as she pushed Luke away from her and walked away. She knew they continued laughing as she stomped down the hall, but had a hard time being mad at them. If the tables were turned, she'd be laughing, too.

She went right to Byron's office. This was the time of day that he did paperwork, so probably not the best time to interrupt him, but she didn't want him getting the wrong idea. She told him the whole story.

"Can you assure me this isn't about feeding?" he asked when she finished.

"Absolutely. I tested myself at his neck and I wasn't tempted."

"You're sure?"

"We kissed. I knew his blood would be delicious, but I was under control. To be careful, I'll make sure I feed right before going out with him. Byron, he's a gentle, funny, wonderful man. And, to be blunt, he's very sexy. I can keep this a human relationship."

"I trust you, Lorna, but Holly may have a problem with it."

"Parker knows we were going out. He's probably already told her, but I'll talk to her myself. If she hates the idea of her brother being with a vampire, I'll back off."

"I have no right to get involved in my employee's personal relationships. It's just the whole situation with Parker and Holly. Chris means so much to her. If she's satisfied, I certainly won't interfere."

"Thank you," Lorna said.

She headed for the steps to go talk to Holly knowing it might be more intimidating than talking to Byron. She didn't expect to find Holly, Parker and Crystal sitting in the common room playing some card game. Oh well, might as well talk to all three at once.

Parker gave her a surprised look, but Holly's expression was pretty unreadable as she asked, "Is this about Chris?"

Lorna was right. Parker had told her. "Holly, I want to reassure you that I won't feed from Chris. He's a great guy and I like spending time with him."

"I was pretty upset when Parker told me," Holly said. "It's just that sometimes I feel like we take advantage of humans and I don't want that to happen to Chris. He's been used before, and he deserves better than that."

"I don't want to use him. I really like him." She wondered what Holly meant that he'd been used before, but wasn't going to ask. "I'm going to be very careful."

"Good," Holly said and tried to smile.

"Holly," Crystal said. "You do realize that Byron will eventually have to tell him about us, don't you? There're too many secrets around here to keep them for long."

"I know," Holly answered quietly. "It's just … I think he'll be upset about me, and he's so happy now."

"And then he'll find out that not only his sister, but his girlfriend are both vampires," Lorna said with concern in her eyes.

"Yeah," Holly said with the same concern in her eyes.

"He's got a lot of strength of character," Lorna said. "It's one of the things I like about him. He'll be able to handle all this."

"Yeah, he's got his shit together," Parker added with a smile. "I think you're right, Lorna. He'll handle it."

Lorna smiled back at him. "I'm going to get some sleep," she said and turned to walk down the hall to her room.

"Lorna," Holly said. "It's not up to me to tell Chris who to date, but I just want him to be protected as long as possible. Thanks for coming to me."

Chapter 5

It bothered me a little as I watched Chris and Lorna spending more and more time together. I admit that I'm sometimes slow at noticing things, but it was almost a week after Chris moved into his apartment that I realized Lorna never came back to Rule the Night until just before dawn.

Lorna was great, and I really liked her, so the only thing that bothered me was that she was a vampire. Otherwise, they looked so happy together, and I was all for anything that made Chris happy. He deserved someone, after the years he'd spent being used by Gretchen.

So I told him I was glad about him being with Lorna, and Parker and I hung out with them sometimes. I was still pretty apprehensive, though, about how he'd react when Byron had to finally tell him the truth about Rule the Night. So strange that both these wonderful guys had girlfriends that could kill them so quickly and viciously.

That was something I couldn't do anything about, and I tried to put all the worries out of my head so I could enjoy seeing Chris every day, spending time with Parker, and being content with how well things were going at Rule the Night. The problem with putting worries aside, though, was that they often had a way of crashing back into your life.

That crash came one night when I called Parker as soon as I woke up from a good day's sleep, but he didn't answer. It was strange. He knew I'd be calling, because I called every day. I told myself that he might have taken Sarita somewhere, and didn't hear his phone.

I showered, dressed, and headed out to see if I could find him. Sarita was in the common room dusting.

"Sorry, Holly," she said, "I haven't seen Parker at all today."

"I'll find him," I smiled at her.

Upstairs, Anna was wheeling the big bucket and mop out of the men's bathroom. I remembered that task very well and didn't miss it. I hated to make a big deal out of it because Parker was certainly allowed to go where he pleased without checking with me, but something about him not answering bothered me. It was a cell phone, for heaven's sake, so he would answer no matter where he was. Maybe Anna had seen him.

"Parker took Clair to New Albany as soon as he got home from school," Anna said. I must have gotten a funny look on my face, because Anna got one, too. "I don't think it's anything to worry about," she added.

"No, I'm not worried." I tried, but I don't think I was able to keep the scowl off my face. "I wonder why they went there."

"Clair said they were going shopping."

"Shopping? All the way to New Albany?"

"Well, I don't think he wanted you to know." My eyebrows raised on that one. "No, no. There's nothing going on. He's been looking for something for you, and she knew a place in New Albany. That's all."

"It's all good," I said with as much of a smile that I could get. "I just wondered why he wasn't answering his phone."

"I'm sure it's nothing," Anna said as she went back to work.

"Yeah, nothing," I said quietly.

Normally, I'm not the jealous or suspicious type, but something about this was making both those feelings swirl around in my brain. What would he be buying that he'd need Clair's help?

Either Crystal or Sarita would have gladly gone with him to buy me something, and they both knew me better. Why Clair?

I really didn't want to even think that there may be something between them, but Parker was a pretty frustrated guy, and Crystal could be very tempting. After all, she'd been a prostitute for a long time. Why would you need to take an ex-ho shopping? Okay, that wasn't very nice thinking of her as a ho, but I wasn't feeling very nice.

He was off somewhere alone with Clair and not answering his phone. Why would he not be answering his phone? What could they be doing? I could imagine what they might be doing, but didn't want my mind to go there.

But maybe if he was buying me something sexy. Something that Parker may be embarrassed to buy himself or with Sarita or Crystal. Something that Clair would have experience with. Was Parker buying me sexy underwear, or a nightie, or something? Oh, jeez! I decided not to think about it anymore.

By midnight, though, we were all worried about Parker and Clair. No one had heard from them, and Parker's cell phone went right to voicemail. We all knew that something was seriously wrong.

TJ had been on his computer to check police reports. I don't know how he could access them, but he did. There were no accidents that could have been them, no reports of any muggings or shootings. Byron called all the hospital emergency rooms between us and New Albany. Nothing!

I was seriously about to lose it, but I wouldn't let myself cry. They'd get home and be fine. They had to. I tried so hard all night to concentrate on serving drinks so I wouldn't let my horrible thoughts drive me nuts. I had to work really hard to fight back the worst thought. What if I never saw Parker again?

No, I couldn't go there. I couldn't let myself think of him lying hurt, or worse, along some road. There were so many horrible things that could happen to someone, and if I let myself think of them, I'd go nuts.

Poor Parker. If he was a vampire, he'd heal quickly from almost any injury. If we just knew where he was, Byron could change him before he died. Oh, God! I couldn't think about that. He'd come back to me and be fine. He had to.

By closing time at 2:00 am, we were all beyond worried. Everyone cared about Parker, and Clair, too, even though she'd only been at Rule the Night a short time. But Byron and I had our hearts tied to Parker like our own lifelines.

All night we'd all been checking with each other for any word, trying to assure each other that he'd be fine and not talking about what could have happened. Byron and I could hardly look at each other. The look on his face drained all my hope and I'm sure my face did the same to him.

We shut down the bar and gathered in Byron's office because there was nothing else any of us could think to do. The extra guards from the Assembly had driven back and forth to New Albany several times hoping to find some trace of them, and TJ kept checking for police and hospital reports. I kept dialing his number every five minutes hoping he'd answer. I don't know how many worried messages I'd left for him.

Anthony, who'd started as guard just a few days before I was sent to Nibble, was at the employee entrance. We all longed to hear from him that the green Bug had pulled into the parking lot or the garage.

"TJ!" Anthony shouted.

We all ran the few steps between Byron's office and the guard's office. Were they back? Could I possibly hope that I'd see Parker stepping out of the green Bug?

Anthony, TJ and Quinton got to the door in time to see a black sedan pull away. I got there soon enough to see a dark body lying on the sidewalk along the edge of the parking lot. My heart dropped into my stomach and I froze. The scent was dead, human blood.

Everyone else ran to the body, but I couldn't make my legs move. I stood paralyzed at the bottom of the outside steps. My hands were on my face covering my nose and mouth, I wasn't breathing, and my brain was shut down. I was nothing. Without Parker, I knew I'd never be anything again.

Byron spun and dashed back toward me. With his vampire speed, he was within inches of me and had his hands on my shoulders in a split second.

"It's not Parker," he gasped.

I still couldn't move. I stared into his eyes wondering if he was real and telling me the truth or was I seeing him and hearing those words like some kind of hallucination. I wanted his words to be true so much I thought I might explode.

"It's not him," he repeated quietly as he hugged me and brought me back to life.

I saw Quinton quickly carrying the body toward the garage. He'd dispose of it somewhere. Everyone else followed TJ toward Byron and me.

"Byron," TJ said quietly, "we found this." TJ held out a piece of paper.

As he read it silently, his expression changed from curiosity, to fear, to rage like I'd never seen on Byron's face before. I was scared. Not of Byron, but of what that note must say that would make his anger seethe through him like that.

He glared at me. "You need to see this," he said with his voice a deep, dark reflection of his anger.

The large, flowing script said:

Byron,

The next body you find on your doorstep will be Parker unless you send me Holly and Luke. The two of them will come alone to Green Lawn Cemetery at midnight on Saturday and wait at the main mausoleum. No negotiations. I get them, and you get Parker.

I knew you would be sentimental enough to take in the poor, helpless Clair. See what compassion for the worthless humans gets you?

Charles

I stared at it long after I finished reading. Charles had Parker. I knew too well what he liked to do to humans, but couldn't stand to think of it.

"Byron," TJ said quietly, "it was Clair's body. She was beaten and drained."

Too much! Too much for my brain to process in any normal way. Charles's atrocities just kept going. He wasn't just bloodthirsty, he was completely insane! If he was capable of doing that to someone who'd been faithful to him for years, what would he do to Parker?

"Let's get inside," Byron said. What else could any of us say?

We stood in Byron's office while the note passed around so everyone could read it. Crystal and I held each other. I was so shocked by all this, I wasn't even crying.

"I'll meet him at the cemetery …" Luke started to say.

"Yeah, I'll go, too," I whispered.

"No!" Byron shouted.

I opened my mouth to argue, but Luke interrupted me. "Holly, Byron's right. You can't go." I glared at him and opened my mouth again.

But Luke interrupted again before I could say anything. "I was going to say that I would go, but we need a bigger plan than that. We know Charles. I'm sorry to say it, but he won't just let Parker walk away. It'll be a trap. We have to find Parker before Saturday."

"Charles's ultimate goal is to take you down, Byron," TJ said. "He's using Parker and he killed Clair as his bait to get to you. Luke's right, we'll have to find him."

"Which is exactly what Charles expects us to do," Quinton added. "The Assembly has had its spies out looking for his club and they think they've found it. Charles probably knows that. Any of us go walking in there, and Parker's dead."

"That's more reason that it has to be me!" I practically shouted. "I'll walk in there and trade myself for Parker." My voice grew quiet and gasped a little. "We all know what he's capable of. I don't care what he does to me. I don't care if he tortures and kills me, as long as Parker's safe."

Every mouth in the room opened to argue with me, but it was the determined, angry voice from the doorway we heard.

"No way in hell!" Chris shouted.

We were all stunned. Chris stood there fuming, glaring at us, but especially at me. "I don't know what the hell's going on here, but you are not going anywhere near this Charles guy. I'll drag your ass out of here and chain you in my closet first." His voice softened a little at the end of his speech.

Lorna stepped to him and put her hand on his shoulder to offer any comfort she could. I don't even know if Chris felt it because he just kept staring at me with more pain in his eyes than the anger that had been there.

"Chris," I gasped. I dashed toward him faster than I intended to and grabbed him in my arms, almost knocking him over. Now I was crying, and everyone else was silent.

"I think we have some explaining to do," Byron said with no emotion.

I turned away from Chris to look at Byron. I gave him a tiny nod, but he got it. He knew I agreed that Chris needed to learn the truth.

"Do you want the guards to leave?" TJ asked Byron.

"No. Chris knows all of us, so we might as well all be part of telling him what he needs to hear."

Chris looked at me as he heard Byron's ominous words. "Holly?" he said. His voice sounded so confused, so scared.

Byron answered before I could. "Chris," he said, "first of all, I would chain Holly in a closet myself before I let her walk into Charles's club. She is not going."

I glared at him. "It is not up for discussion, Holly," he said while glaring back. "Chris, what are you doing here after hours?"

"I was coming around the building to wait for Lorna when I saw all of you outside. The door was open, and I just followed you in. So, what's going on here?"

"There's a lot going on that you don't know about," Byron said. "I think you should sit down while I explain some things. It will take some time."

I remembered my thoughts when I first realized that there were secrets at Rule the Night. Drugs, prostitution, gangster stuff had all flown through my head, and I was sure Chris was thinking some of the same things.

I sat in the chair next to him and held his hand while Byron began to explain. When he said the word "vampire" Chris's grip tightened on my hand and he started to shake. I reached out with my other hand so I was holding his with both of mine.

As Byron briefly recounted the story of my attack and change, I felt Chris move. It was like he was subconsciously pulling away from me. I felt his fear spike as he realized that all the people around him, all the people he worked with and thought he knew, were vampires. Even his little sister.

I remembered how scared I was when Byron and Parker told me, yet Chris just sat there listening. He'd started out looking at Byron, but now was staring down at the desk between them. I don't think he even blinked.

Then Byron told him about my history with Charles and Nibble. Chris snapped his head toward me and stared with fear, disbelief and sadness in his eyes. What must he be thinking? Finally, we got to what was happening tonight.

"Holly ..." Chris was finally ready to say something. "You've been through all this ... I didn't have any idea."

"I know. It's okay," I answered and squeezed his hand.

His eyes held so much sorrow. "The night you came to the apartment asking to stay with Gretchen and me ... that's the night you were attacked? It happened because I turned you away." He looked devastated.

"No! That wasn't your fault! I shouldn't have been out there. I should have trusted Byron and Parker. It was all my fault!"

He hugged me and buried his face in my shoulder. "You would have been safe if I'd let you stay."

There was so much anguish in his quiet voice. "But I wouldn't have had Parker and this life at Rule the Night. I'm happy here, happier than my human life ever was."

He pulled back and looked in my eyes. He was getting it. I wasn't human anymore. None of us were human.

He stared at me a moment, then turned to look up at Lorna. "You, too," he said quietly.

"Yes. I'm a vampire," Lorna said very matter-of-factly.

"Have you drunk my blood?"

"No. I swore to Byron and Holly that I wouldn't feed from you."

"But, we've been alone almost every night at my place. Byron said Holly couldn't resist Parker …"

"We're all different, Chris. Different things make us lose control. I admit I've been tempted, but I've been able to control myself. I have *not* fed from you."

He reached up and took her hand, and I knew he was starting to accept this bizarre situation. He held both my hands with one of his and Lorna's with the other. I started to feel that Chris was going to be okay. He went back to staring down at the desk, but it was going to take a little while to be comfortable with the fact that the two people he cared for the most were not human, but both vampires. I had no idea what he was thinking.

"We have to make some decisions about Charles," Byron finally said.

I knew how anxious he was about Parker. As much as I was emotionally all tied up with Chris's feelings right now, the thought of Parker being Charles's victim never left me for a second.

"You're welcome to stay, Chris, or you can go," Byron continued. "I know this is a lot to think about and you might need some time. You'll have questions and you should feel free to ask any of us what you want to know."

"Yeah, man," Luke said, "full disclosure mode. Ask us anything."

Chris actually found a small smile for him.

"If I understood everything right," Chris started hesitantly, "people go to places like Rule the Night and vampires drink their blood without them knowing about it."

"Yes," Byron said while I nodded. Down deep, part of me still couldn't feel good about it.

"Then I think that makes me the best one to go in there and see if I can get any information about Parker."

"No!" I gasped as Lorna just gasped without words. Byron calmly said, "No way," while shaking his head. And Luke almost smiled muttering, "You've got a hell of a set on you, buddy."

"What?" Chris asked like it was no big deal. "I can handle myself pretty well, and this Charles guy doesn't know me. I'll just be another guy in a bar."

"You have no idea what you'd be facing in there. Anything could happen, and you'd never see it coming," Byron said. "Besides, a strange human that walked in probably wouldn't be able to learn anything."

"But ..." Lorna said like she was getting a brilliant idea. "What if he went in as a vampire's human lover? The two of us could check in for a few days and might be able to learn something."

Chris looked up at Lorna like that was a good idea. Byron's brows grew together like he actually might be considering it.

"Charles doesn't know you?" he asked Lorna.

"I've never met any of the ones you've mentioned. You know I've lived in Europe for the last couple centuries," she looked down at Chris with an apologetic half smile. His eyes got huge at the revelation of how old she must be. "He'll have no way of tying me to you or the Assembly. I'll be the spy, and Chris will be safe as my cover."

"Byron, you can't be seriously considering this," I practically begged. "You can't send Chris in there."

"I don't like it, Holly, but who among us would be safer? Charles would never expect us to send him clients to get information. It could work."

"Chris, don't do it." This time I did beg.

"I want to help get Parker back … for you," Chris answered. "I know how much you love each other, and I want you to be happy."

There were tears in my eyes. "Is it because you feel guilty about not letting me in that night?"

"No," he shook his head. "You're so different since you left Mom and Dad, and I don't think it's because of the vampire thing. I think it's because you're happy. I want you to stay that way."

"Before we go any farther with this," Quinton said while Chris and I hugged, "we need to find out if the Assembly's sure about Charles's location. And we'll need more than just the two of them."

"Exactly," Byron said as he picked up his phone.

We all knew he was calling Constance, the head of the Vampire Assembly. Even though it felt like we were in this alone, I knew the Assembly had been working hard against Charles and they would give us all the help we could ask for. They might even have someone already in the club watching for Charles. It might be his club, but he knew he couldn't casually show himself in public.

"Byron," TJ said before he could punch in his speed dial to Constance. "It's been bothering me that Charles has given us four days before he wants Holly and Luke. It might be that he wants us to have time to try a rescue, but it could also be that he has other plans. Maybe to take someone else. I think we all need to stick close. Both humans and vampires."

"Chris is outside alone every night," I said. The shock of the danger he'd been in made my heart feel like it stopped.

"Exactly," TJ nodded. "But thankfully, Charles doesn't even know Chris exists."

Byron rubbed that spot between his brows. "Chris, you're off valet service until this is solved. We'll need two vampires out there, and you'll have to stay here. You're too vulnerable in your apartment."

"He can stay with me," Lorna said. Chris looked back and forth between them.

"Anthony and I will get cameras on the lot across the street," TJ said, "and it wouldn't hurt to have two of us on the front door."

"Good. And no one else is allowed outside alone. I'll explain something to the clients tonight. They know there's an issue with bloodthirst, so it won't be hard to convince them."

My insides were all screwed up. Not only did Charles have Parker, Chris was going to be at his secret sanctuary. I couldn't let myself think about what I'd seen Charles do to other humans or what he'd done to Clair. It was all too much and happening way too fast.

I looked at Chris and could see how tired and overwhelmed he was. Hard enough to learn the reality of vampires, but all this danger, fear, and plotting had to have his mind spinning. Top that off with the revelation that Lorna and I were also vampires and what might be happening to Parker? I shook my head, not allowing myself to think about that right now.

"Are you hungry Chris?" I asked.

"Starving," he answered blankly.

"I'll show you the kitchen."

"I'll come along if you don't mind, Holly," Lorna said.

"That'd be good," I answered.

We got up to leave and that started others leaving. Everyone had jobs to do or needed to get some sleep. Dawn wasn't far away, and we wouldn't be able to do anything until dark. Crystal hugged me and went over to lean against Byron's desk as he picked up the phone again. TJ and Quinton moved to the side to let others out.

This had been an incredibly long night and I was so, so tired, but I knew I wouldn't be able to sleep. The best thing for me to do was to take care of Chris. He needed me and it would help keep my deepest fears for Parker tucked inside. I would face those later when I was alone.

Chapter 6

Chris ate a cold meatloaf sandwich and drank a beer while Lorna and I held our breaths. I remembered Parker telling me he and Sarita had a great meatloaf dinner the other night, and my stomach clenched at the thought. Not because of the food, but because I let myself think about Parker. I had to keep him out of my head until I was alone or I'd lose it.

We showed Chris downstairs and he was amazed just like I was the first time I saw it. He couldn't believe my room, but I only pointed at Parker's door. I couldn't go in there right now.

"Don't you and Parker live together?" he asked, looking surprised.

"No," I whispered. Inside I wanted to beg Chris not to make me think about why Parker and I couldn't be together.

Chris looked at me a little confused, and Lorna came to my rescue. "I think it's too hard for Holly to talk about him right now. I'll tell you later," she said.

"Sorry, little sis," he said. "I should have realized you wouldn't want to talk about him."

I loved when he called me that. When we were kids, he used that pet name for me all the time and it was somehow comforting to hear him using it again.

"It's okay," I said. "I'm really tired. I'm going to bed."

"You okay alone?" he asked. "I can stay with you."

"I think I need some time alone. I'll see you tomorrow." I turned to go into my room, but Chris touched my shoulder to stop me.

"Hey, you know Byron better than I do, but I get the feeling he's not someone you want as an enemy. Don't worry too much, okay?" Chris reached out and hugged me. "He'll get Parker back."

I nodded. "Yeah. He will. Goodnight."

"G'night," they both said.

I closed the door behind me and stretched out on my bed without even taking off my shoes. Then I cried my heart out.

* * *

Lorna showed Chris into her room.

"Nice," he said as he looked around. "Byron treats you guys well."

"Very well. I have to go see if TJ needs anything before I sleep. The bathroom's through there if you want to shower."

"You're leaving?" A little fear showed in Chris's eyes.

"I'll only be an hour or so."

"Before you go, can I hold you for a minute?" Lorna put her arms around him, and he buried his face in her neck. "Lorna, this is all too much. It's just rolling around in my brain, and I can't make any sense of it."

"I know," she whispered as she stroked his back.

"I gotta' tell you, I'd be scared to death, but ... it's you and Holly. And all these people I've gotten to know. I mean, I like all of them. I don't know what to think."

"I think you're overwhelmed. You need time to let it settle, and you need some sleep. Crawl in and I'll join you when I get back."

Chris raised his head to look in her eyes. "The whole vampire thing. Are you going to drink my blood, now that I know?"

"I don't think Byron or Holly would object, but it'd be completely your choice."

"Does it hurt?"

"I can make it not hurt, and your blood would be incredibly delicious. We'd both enjoy it."

"I don't know." He looked away from her.

"I'm not asking. I won't feed from you unless you want it."

"I'll think about it."

"Not tonight. Sleep, and we'll talk about all the questions you have. But right now, I have to go."

"I'll wait up for you." They kissed gently and Chris was left alone with his thoughts.

He showered hoping to get stuff out of his head, but it didn't seem to help much. He went through the motions with a strangely blank mind and found himself standing in his boxer shorts, staring into the mirror.

How could all of this have been going on around him while he didn't have a clue? The important thing, though, was that Parker made Holly happy. Happier than she'd ever been before. Chris couldn't just stand by and let her lose that happiness because some monster kidnapped Parker.

Chris hadn't realized how sad and scared Holly used to look until he saw her everyday at Rule the Night. This life, these people, and especially Parker made Holly a different person, and he couldn't stand for her to lose what she'd found. No matter how dangerous it was, Chris would do everything he could to help get Parker back for her.

He finally climbed into Lorna's bed and snuggled under the soft comforter. Chris buried his face in her pillow and smelled Lorna's special smell. Warm, woodsy, almost dark. It was how Lorna always smelled and he couldn't get enough of it. Thinking of her instead of everything he'd learned tonight, Chris quickly fell into a deep sleep.

When Lorna came back, she showered and climbed in beside him. He was sound asleep, so she just wrapped her arms around him and hoped sleep would come quickly. It didn't, though, because she couldn't stop worrying about Chris.

He'd looked so scared, so lost when he asked to hold her. He'd had to face so much tonight, and Lorna wanted to help him sort through it, but she really didn't know how.

She was afraid to take him to such a dangerous sanctuary. He had no experience with the world they would be walking into, and she'd have to keep a very close eye on him. At the same time, try to convince the vampires in charge that she was interested in bloodthirst.

If Chris was hurt, or heaven's forbid killed, she'd never be able to face Holly or Byron. And she'd never forgive herself. Chris was becoming too important to her, so she'd have to keep him safe or die trying.

Chris stirred, but didn't wake up. He mumbled in his sleep, rolled toward her, and wrapped his arm across her waist. Snuggling against her and burying his face into her neck, he let out a deep sigh of contentment. Yes, she would keep him safe at all costs.

* * *

I rolled off the bed about 2:00 that afternoon. I hadn't slept at all. After crying and sobbing for hours, I'd just stretched out on my back and looked toward the dark ceiling. I felt so helpless. So worried. Worried about Parker's safety. Worried about Chris's safety. Underneath all that, I still worried about the idea of Parker being willing to go off with Clair. Was I being ridiculous?

He had so many good reasons to leave me. I tried to kill him. Who would stay with a fiancé that he had to be afraid of? A fiancé that he could barely even kiss. A fiancé that was getting intimate with strange guys every few nights. Could I really blame him for going off with someone else?

What I wanted more than anything was to walk into that sanctuary, kill Charles with my bare hands, and carry Parker out. But I couldn't do any of that. I wasn't powerful enough, strong enough, to face Charles. Even if Byron would let me go, I'd be no help at all.

There was nothing I could do to stop Chris. He'd go with Lorna because he trusted her, wanted me to be happy, and did care about Parker's safety. What could I possibly do except hope for good news? Finally, it dawned on me. If I couldn't directly help Parker, maybe I could help Chris.

I went to Parker's suite. As his scent hit my nostrils, my tears flowed freely again, but I ignored them. Only Byron, Parker, and I knew that there was a gun in the desk drawer. Byron had given it to Parker several years ago in case he was attacked.

It was small and easy to shoot, but the bullets were designed to expand on impact to create a big, bloody wound. It wasn't easy to kill a vampire with a gun, but you could sure slow them down, hopefully enough to get away.

I picked up the gun, shoulder holster, and extra bullets. Parker had never had to use it, and I prayed that Chris wouldn't either. Regardless, he'd have it if he needed it.

I went into Parker's huge walk-in closet. The fact that it was half empty made me even sadder than I already was. The empty parts were waiting for me to move in. Was that ever going to happen? I hated that I now had to face the fact that it might not.

I pulled a small suitcase off the shelf and started packing dressier clothes that would be appropriate for the human lover of a wealthy, powerful vampire. Chris and Parker were about the same size, but I thought Chris was a little more muscular, so I chose the looser, less form-fitting things.

The scent of Parker was overwhelming me to the point that it was hard to see through my tears. But I kept going. Chris needed this, and I had to help this whole plan succeed any way I could.

When finished, I knocked on Lorna's door, and she answered almost immediately, so I stepped in and sat the suitcase on the floor. Chris was still sound asleep in the crumpled bed. He looked so much younger and helpless like that.

"Chris will need clothes, so I packed some of Parker's for him," I whispered. "There's also a gun in there ... just in case."

"Thank you," she whispered back, "I hadn't thought of that."

"Take care of him, Lorna."

"I'll protect him with my life."

There was nothing else to be said. I glanced again at his peaceful face on the pillow, and went back to my own room. Losing Parker and Chris at the same time would be more than I could survive.

The afternoon went faster than I could imagine, but most of it was a blank to me. All I could do was wait to say goodbye to Chris. No! Not goodbye. I wouldn't be able to stand saying that.

We gathered in Byron's office for final instructions and to go through the plans one last time. Besides Lorna, Chris, and me, TJ, Quinton, Luke and Anthony all listened to Byron's every word.

"The Assembly called in reservations for you at Charles's club. It's called Thirst," Byron told Lorna. "If they trace the call, it will look like it came from Indianapolis. They also planted records to make it look like you'd been in Indy for a week.

"If asked, tell them you just found Chris in Indianapolis after spending centuries in Europe. Keep to the truth as much as possible in case they trace you.

"Chris, trust that Lorna knows what she's doing and that she'll protect you. But, whatever you do, stay close to her. Don't let anyone else get you alone, don't talk about her, and act as if you are completely devoted to her."

"I'll treat him as if I'm a jealous shrew and snarl at anyone that gets near him," Lorna said smiling at Chris.

I think Chris would have smiled back if he hadn't been so nervous. I could tell he was really scared, too. If I didn't trust Lorna, I'd grab him and carry him as far away from all this as I could. He said he wanted to do it, but I knew deep inside that was because he felt guilty about not letting me stay with him and Gretchen that night.

He was doing this for me, which brought back those old feelings that a big brother should protect his little sister. The truth was, though, that I was now much more capable of taking care of him. I wanted to protect him from all this, but it was too late for that now. I'd have to trust Lorna to take care of him for me.

Too soon, Lorna and Chris were ready to leave. Everyone had said the "good luck", and "see you soon" lines while avoiding that dreaded goodbye. We were all being very brave and optimistic.

The Assembly had given us the address and directions to Thirst, and warned that it was in a very rough part of Columbus. The area was filled with old, empty warehouses, abandoned trucking companies, vacant factories, and some possible meth labs. I was scared to death for them.

We all watched them pull out of the garage and down the alley on their way to Columbus, and I lost it. I sobbed into my hands and shook from head to toes.

Byron put his arm around my shoulders. "Come, Holly," he said quietly.

He walked me down the stairs into his suite, led me to the huge over-stuffed couch, and sat down next to me without ever moving his arm from my shoulders. We hugged and I cried my eyes out on his shoulder for quite a while.

Finally, I found enough voice to speak. "I gave Chris some of Parker's clothes … and his gun." My face was still on Byron's shoulder, so I'm sure my words were pretty muffled, but I wasn't ready to look at him, yet.

"Lorna told me."

"She's going to keep him safe," I mumbled.

"She's very strong and determined, Holly. You don't need to worry about Chris."

"I know."

"And we'll find Parker. He'll be back with you, with all of us, as soon as possible."

I hesitated and whispered very quietly, "If he wants to come back to me."

Byron moved me from his shoulder and his confused eyes met mine. "Why would you say that?"

"It's complicated," I shook my head, not wanting to tell him what I was thinking.

"Holly, please tell me. Did you two have a disagreement?"

"No … it's just … everything's different since I came back from Chicago."

"How is it different?"

"You've seen it! He treats me like Crystal or Sarita. Like a friend, not a girlfriend!" So much had been rattling around in my head and eating away at my heart. Now that I was actually putting all my thoughts and fears into words, I was practically yelling.

"But, Holly …"

"I tried to kill him! He saw that beast in my eyes! How could he still love me? Most of the time, I think he's afraid to touch me!"

"I think he's being patient and …"

"Oh, Byron," I interrupted him again, "I tried to kill him, and he's afraid I'll do it again. He's afraid of me!"

"Holly!" Byron didn't yell. He gave me that quiet, scary voice of authority that he was so good at. "Stop talking and listen to me! You didn't scare Parker at all. Even as he was losing consciousness, he was sure you were going to stop. When he woke after the transfusions, he was still sure you would have stopped. It was TJ that scared the crap out of him and made him realize that he was being childish. Believe me, Holly, he loves you very much. Enough to stay away from you until he's changed."

"Then why did he run off with Clair?" I shouted through my sobs.

"Is that what you think?"

"It's what happened! Anna could hardly look me in the eye when she said he was with Clair."

"Holly, sweetheart … Clair fooled us all. Clair offered to go with him to a jewelry store in New Albany because he was looking for an engagement ring for you. He couldn't find anything he liked in Adelle."

"Really?"

"Yes!" His voice was so determined and assured. "He complained to all of us that he couldn't find a ring for you. I think she and Charles used that information to get him alone."

"I thought he left me," I sobbed. Byron hugged me again.

"He loves you, Holly. He hasn't looked at anyone else since he met you. When you gave him that picture, he told me that he wished he could tell his parents about you. He thinks the two of you have the kind of love they had."

"Oh, Byron, I love him so much!" I gasped through my tears.

"I know. And we'll get him back."

Chapter 7

Lorna drove the two hours to Charles's club answering every question Chris had. Nine hours of sleep had done wonders for him, and he wanted to know everything. The thing he wanted the most, though, was to understand exactly what bloodthirst was.

"It's not really one thing," Lorna said. "Charles chose bloodthirst. That kind is sadistic and cruel. It has more to do with terrifying and sometimes torturing, less to do with feeding, although, the victim is eventually drained."

"Is that what Holly saw in Chicago?" he asked.

"Uh huh. That's what she saw."

"And what those two tried to do to her."

"Yes."

"Man. Poor Holly."

"What happened with Holly and Parker, though, is a different kind. The sudden, strong smell of human blood can shock us into a loss of control. Reacting to raw instinct, the vampire attacks and can't stop feeding. They don't mean to kill, but can't stop. It happens more easily with younger vampires like Holly, but even very old ones can lose control to it."

"She thinks it was her fault, doesn't she?"

"And Parker's scent still tempts her. That's why they never spend any time alone."

"That's sad. You can see how much they love each other. Parker can't stop talking about her. He's always asking me what she was like as a kid," Chris smiled.

"It is sad," Lorna nodded. "Sometimes we run into a blood scent that is worse than all the others. Maybe it has to do with them caring about each other before she was changed, I don't know."

They were quiet for a while. "There's a third kind of bloodthirst, but it's one we don't see often anymore," Lorna eventually continued. "When a new vampire is changed quickly and allowed to drain their first donor, it's hard for them to find the control they need to not kill. The more they kill, the harder it is to stop."

"How do you stop them from killing the first one?"

"You have to physically open their jaws and pull them off the donor."

"It's that intense?"

"Yes. Until a couple hundred years ago, we all killed and had to learn the control we needed on our own. It was hard, but most of us made it and haven't killed since."

"You used to kill humans?" Chris sounded almost dumbfounded. He couldn't see Lorna killing.

"Yes. So did Byron and TJ. The whole issue we're fighting now is that some want to go back to the old ways. Those are the vampires that are drawn to Charles and his kind of sadistic bloodthirst. Charles is one of the worst, though, because he seems to believe that we're better than humans and they deserve to die. He's not out of control at all. He likes to kill because he thinks he has a right to."

"He's insane," Chris murmured.

"I think so," Lorna answered. "Looks like we're here."

Chris looked up at the grungy, steel walls of what used to be a warehouse. It would still look abandoned if it weren't for the light over the obviously heavy-duty front door. The door was wide open as someone was allowed in, and it had a guard on each side.

Loud, hard music blasted from inside, and he could see the lights were dim.

"Man, this looks like a rough place. I've been in some sleazy bars before, but not this bad."

"Hopefully the vampire areas will be better."

"Well, damn," Chris said, "a valet's coming for the car."

"I'm thinking they hide the main parking out back to avoid anyone noticing how many customers they have."

"Slick."

"You ready?" Lorna looked at Chris with her eyebrows raised.

"Ready or not ..." he answered with a grin as the valet approached the car.

Lorna popped the trunk and left the car running. The valet lifted out their bags and handed her a claim ticket.

"Clients enter through the side entrance," the valet said indicating the right side of the building.

"Thank you," Lorna answered as Chris picked up their bags.

"How did he know you were a client?" Chris whispered, as they walked away.

Lorna winked at him. "He could smell what I am," she said quietly.

They walked to the side of the building to face another pair of guards.

"We have reservations," Lorna said.

"This way," one guard said and led them inside.

They followed him into a small entryway that made a sharp, right turn toward the back of the building to continue down a narrow hallway. At the end was a tall desk with another guard standing behind it.

"Lorna and guest from Indianapolis," she said, and handed over a piece of paper with a confirmation number.

The guard opened a door next to his desk to reveal a wide stairway. "You have Room 27," he said. "Third door down the right hallway."

He handed them a keycard and sent them on their way. Chris noticed he never smiled, never said anything like a welcome, and barely looked at them. The employees of the cheapest hotel Gretchen had ever taken him at least did that much.

At the bottom of the stairs was a common room like at Rule the Night, only not as big and not furnished. Room 27 was like any hotel, double bed, not queen or king, dresser with a TV on top, small bathroom, small closet.

"Not the Ritz, is it?" Chris said looking around.

Lorna grinned. "Charles went cheap on this one. Let's get upstairs and get on with it. We can unpack later."

"Let's go," Chris sighed like he was preparing himself for the performance of his life.

"Whatever happens, Chris, just follow my lead and stay close to me."

They took a small table for two in a corner, and Chris was surprised that the people in the bar were such a mixture of types. Some were well dressed and pretty classy looking, and others were as rough as he expected them to be judging from the outside of the place. Of course, he reminded himself, not all of them were people.

Lorna started sorting through them as they looked around the room and pointed out to Chris which ones were vampires and which were human. Almost all the classier ones were the vampires.

"So, what do we do now?" Chris asked.

"Watch," she answered with a shrug. Then she leaned close to him and whispered, "Byron showed me pictures of some suspects.

You watch how things work and who leaves for private rooms." As she started to move back, she briefly kissed his lips.

Chris smiled and put his arm around her shoulders. "I forgot we need to make it obvious that we're together," he whispered back.

Lorna smiled and ordered as a waitress stopped at their table – a beer for Chris and water for herself. Then they watched the crowd and talked quietly about nothing. Chris watched vampires and humans approach each other and walk off into an area behind the bar. A while later, they came back and separated.

It was pretty obvious what was going on, but he could tell that if he didn't know this was a place for vampires to feed he wouldn't have noticed. He'd gone to a lot of bars with Gretchen. Had they been in a vampire club before? They'd never gone to Rule the Night, so maybe not. But she had taken him to some pretty seedy places. *Hell*, he thought as he realized he might have fed a vampire and never known.

"Are most vampire places like this one, or like Rule the Night?" he asked quietly.

"Most are somewhere in between, but they can be anything. There are some, especially in the largest cities, that are not sanctuaries, but human bars that quite a few vampires frequent."

"Where do they go to feed?"

"Bathrooms, parking lot, wherever they can find some privacy."

Lorna leaned into Chris's neck again. "The one who just sat at the end of the bar is named Randall. He's one I've been watching for."

"Why don't I wander over to get another beer?" he said into her ear. "Maybe I can hear something."

"Be careful," she frowned.

Chris grabbed his empty bottle and walked around the dance floor to get to the end of the bar where the stranger was talking to the bartender. All he heard was general comments about it being a good crowd tonight before the bartender looked at him. The look was raised eyebrows that asked what he wanted while seeming to be irritated by the interruption.

Chris smiled like he didn't even notice the irritation and sat the empty on the bar. "Bud and a club soda," he said.

The bartender grabbed the beer from under the counter and drew the club soda from the tap without saying a word. Placing them on the bar in front of Chris, he said, "6.25."

"Put it on Room 27." Chris picked up their drinks, said, "Nice place you've got here," and headed back to Lorna.

"Nothing," he shrugged as he sat down.

"Maybe something," she said as she looked past him to where Randall was heading through the crowd toward them. "Look who's coming over."

"Excuse me, Lorna. May I join you?" Randall said as he got to them.

"Of course," Lorna gave him a tiny grin that was really just a pleasant face. Chris wondered what she was really thinking.

"I hear you've recently returned to us after being in Europe for several years," Randall said casually as he pulled over another chair.

Lorna laughed quietly, not a genuine laugh at all. "Seems you know quite a bit about me, and I don't know you at all."

"I apologize. My name is Randall. What brings you back to the states?"

"Boredom."

"With all the lovely sanctuaries throughout Europe?"

"One can only take so much refinement."

"And Indianapolis didn't please you?"

"Well, I did meet this adorable man." She turned away from Randall slightly and stroked Chris's cheek.

Chris was amazed by the whole thing, and seeing another side of Lorna. She was being cold, arrogant, and evasive, revealing just enough to Randall to keep him interested. It was like the two of them were waging a verbal battle.

"What made you choose Thirst?"

"I overheard a conversation that intrigued me. I got the impression that Thirst offered a different kind of old world charm."

"Is that what you're looking for?"

"Don't all of us sometimes miss the amusements of our youth?"

"So we do. I hope you both enjoy your time here. I'll tell the bartender Chris's next beer is on the house."

"Thank you."

Randall stood up, gave Lorna a nod that was almost a bow, and left. He went through the door that led to the hallway and downstairs.

"Okay …" Chris said. "I'm not sure I got all that."

"He knows that I'm older than him, so I was changed before the Assembly established its rules," she whispered against his neck. "I tried to give him just enough of a hint that I was looking for something. An old style of feeding."

"Oh. How does he know how old you are?"

"With age, comes strength and power. We smell it on each other."

"Really?"

"Did you notice he leaned toward me when he sat down? He was smelling me."

"So you told him what you wanted, and he said he hoped you enjoyed it here, hinting that you might find what you want."

"Exactly. Let's dance."

The band was playing something slow and dreamy. After a few moments of swaying across the floor with Lorna in his arms, Chris found it possible to let all his fears and worries get pushed to the back of his mind. He was starting to care more and more about Lorna and couldn't stop thinking about her, especially as he held her so close.

She was amazing in so many ways. She was strong and independent, yet sweet and funny. He just plain liked spending time with her more than most of the friends he'd ever had. And, man, they were amazing together in bed. Chris thought making love to Gretchen was great, but Lorna was so much more. Probably because he and Lorna actually cared for each other.

That was another thing he loved, that she wasn't afraid to let him know in a million little ways that she cared about him. Since he learned the truth, he tried to tell himself that he should be afraid of her, but he just couldn't be.

She was strong enough to break him in half, could control him with a glance of her eyes, and could drain every drop of blood from his body while he would be helpless to stop her. But he trusted her. Vampire or not, she was a good person and would never hurt him. He knew that with all his heart.

As the dance ended, Chris leaned in and kissed her. "We should dance more often," he said quietly.

She smiled and led him back to the table. They found a fresh bottle of Bud and a new club soda waiting. Randall must have had them sent over.

"Lorna," Chris said after getting his mind back on the business at hand, "I've noticed something." The music was again loud enough for them to talk quietly without being overheard. "I saw one of the door guards bring a girl in that looked like she was already wasted."

"Where is she?" Lorna asked.

"That's just it. He sat her at the bar and got her a drink. Then another guy came over and took her into the hall that leads downstairs. That was a couple hours ago, and she hasn't come back."

"Are you sure?"

"Pretty sure. I could have missed her, but she was kinda' hard to miss. Light blonde hair with black roots, bright pink tube top, and a really short skirt. I think I would have seen her."

Lorna gazed ahead with a worried look on her face.

"You think something bad happened?" Chris asked.

"It might have."

"Damn it! I wish I'd watched her closer."

"That wouldn't have made a difference, Chris. We know what's going on here, and we didn't come to stop it. We wouldn't be able to if we had."

"It just makes me mad as hell. I mean, she could be … gone."

"I know. That's what we're fighting."

Chris put his arm back around her and they sat silently watching the crowd. Finally, it was close to dawn and few customers and clients were still around. The band announced last song, and Chris and Lorna headed downstairs to their room.

"I expected them to close earlier than dawn," Chris said, yawning.

"So did I. Legally, they'd have to, but there's not much that's legal in this place."

They closed the door to their room and could talk privately, but they still kept their voices quiet.

"Did we get anywhere tonight?" Chris asked.

"I don't know. If Randall caught my hints, which I'm sure he did, he'll probably try to check me out. He won't find any evidence of bloodthirst in Europe, but that won't mean much. I would have hidden it very carefully. I just hope he doesn't find anything to connect me to Byron or the Assembly."

There was a light knock on their door. Lorna raised her eyebrows and went to answer it. Randall smiled and asked her to step out to the common room with him.

"Get ready for bed, Chris. I'll be right back."

Lorna's voice had sounded commanding and cold, but Chris was suddenly scared to death for her. What did Randall want? If they hurt her, there was nothing he could do about it. He needed a plan.

Opening his suitcase, he pulled the gun out from under his clothes, and placed it on top where he could get it quickly. Checking his phone to see if he had a signal this deep underground, he nodded to himself as he saw four bars. If anything went wrong, he'd shoot first and call Byron second.

Then he stood with his hand on the gun as he waited. Within a few minutes, the door opened, Lorna stepped in, and leaned her back against the door as she closed it. The look on her face was a strange combination of fear, accomplishment, and something else he couldn't identify.

"He offered me a human that would be unaccounted for," she said quietly.

"What did you say?"

"I pretended to be torn between my two choices, then told him I was more in the mood for you today. But I accepted his offer for later."

"They have a human for you to kill." Chris was disgusted.

"That's what he was offering."

"That girl that never came back to the bar?"

"Probably not. They would usually have a male for me."

"Parker?"

"No. If Charles wanted him dead, he'd do it himself to hurt Byron."

"What are you going to do?"

"I'll have to come up with some excuse, but whatever happens, I'm not going to be tempted into bloodthirst," she said with determination. Then added quietly, "He didn't make me that hungry."

Chris moved toward Lorna with intentions of hugging her. She moved across the room keeping distance between them and turned away from him.

"What's wrong? You look upset," Chris said.

"He took me out there to test me. Another vampire was feeding, and the scent of human blood was strong. I need a minute."

Chris realized what that strange look on her face was. He'd never seen her without her usual steely control. Randall had tried to make her lose it, and now he was alone in here with her. She'd told him what a great temptation the scent of blood could be and how a vampire, even one as old as she was, could lose control. He didn't know what to do, so he just stood there and stared at her back.

"Should I leave?" he finally asked quietly.

"No," she turned and smiled. Her expression was more relaxed, but still determined. "I'm okay, now." She hesitated. "Don't be afraid, Chris. I'll never feed from you unless you want it."

Now it was Chris's turn to hesitate and question what he wanted to say. But he had to say it. "When we were dancing, I decided I want it. I want to know what it's like." Then he hesitated again while she stared at him. "I want you to bite me," he whispered.

"Are you sure? You're not saying that because you think I want it, or it's hard for me to resist you?"

"Is it hard for you to resist me?" he murmured with a sexy grin.

"Always," she whispered back.

Chris couldn't wait anymore. With his arms around her waist, he pulled her against him and kissed her. They held on to each other as the kiss got more passionate. He was sure. He wanted all of Lorna, and she was a vampire. He'd never know her until he experienced her bite.

Chris looked into her eyes. "You said it wouldn't hurt, and we'd both enjoy it?"

"Yes."

"Then why haven't you done it?"

"I wanted it to be your choice. I'm here because I care about you, not because I need to be fed. I don't need your blood to make me happy, Chris. I need you."

"Oh, man," Chris sighed. "Do it, Lorna. Do it."

Lorna gazed into his eyes before kissing him. Her lips moved to the corner of his mouth, to the short whiskers on his jaw, and finally to his neck. Her fangs extended through her gums as she licked that spot under his ear and let herself feel the blood flowing through his veins. She hesitated, giving him the chance to change his mind. Looking again into his eyes, she knew he was a little scared but determined.

As she bit into his flesh, he gasped slightly from the surprise, then sighed sweetly as he relaxed into the sensation. His blood tasted glorious, as Lorna knew it would, but she had gained enough control not to do a full feeding. She just had a taste. Finishing, she stroked his neck with her tongue, closing the wound from her teeth.

Chris had stood perfectly still except for his hands which stroked and kneaded the muscles of her back and her hair. She kissed his neck and moved back to his mouth.

"How was it?" she whispered against his lips.

"Relaxing, yet … hot as hell," he murmured. "Did you control how I felt?"

"No. I just took away the pain."

"Believe me, I'm feeling no pain," Chris grinned. "You can do that again whenever you want."

Lorna smiled, "I'll surprise you."

Chris hugged her tighter, wondering what he'd been so afraid of. "Join me in a shower?" he whispered against her neck.

"Love to," she answered.

Chapter 8

Parker woke feeling like he'd been in the middle of a strange dream. No, a nightmare. Or maybe he was still in it. Trying to look around, he realized that it was absolutely black. He thought about trying to move, but wasn't sure if he should or if he could.

Everything was wrong. There were strange bits of memories in his head, but he couldn't fit any of them together in any way that made sense. Pain, fear, screams, hunger. Which ones were his, which ones did he witness? Maybe he'd figure it out if he could get anything to make sense.

Where was this place? How long had he been here? It could be minutes, hours, or days, but Parker had no idea. No, he felt like it had been a while. Seemed like there were too many disjointed memories of things for it to have all happened quickly.

As he sat up, the room swayed, but it was some progress at least. His eyes must have adjusted to the darkness, because he could make out some things. A small room, only about 10x10, with the cot he sat on and one chair. That was it. He'd been in this room for a while. He had a dim vision of half waking here before.

This time, though, Parker thought he had it more together. This time he was remembering stuff. But the memories were almost like a picture book he had to go through one page at a time. If he tried to put the images together, he lost them.

Holly. He remembered Holly and how much they loved each other. He remembered driving with Clair, but thinking about Holly the whole time. He remembered stopping along the road. He remembered the screams.

The memories came faster and suddenly started to fit together. They were attacked by a huge vampire, even bigger than TJ, who paralyzed him and left him standing there. *Oh, God*, Parker thought as he dropped his head into his hands. That vampire attacked Clair and left Parker standing there to watch.

Now it was all like a horrible movie playing before his eyes. The vampire. Charles. He remembered that it was Charles. He beat Clair, holding her by the throat as his fists flew at her face and body. He threw her down on the side of the road, kicked her over and over, and finally drank her blood until her lifeless body hung like a rag across his arm. Then Charles dropped her and turned toward Parker.

Parker closed his eyes again as he sat on the side of the cot hoping to avoid the vision of Charles's face. But it was in his head and closing his eyes wouldn't make it go away. Charles's fangs and his crazy eyes came closer and closer while Parker was frozen to the spot, unable to move or scream.

Those eyes. Filled with rage and a strange delight and satisfaction at what he was about to do, yet, also filled with disgust and revulsion. Parker could see it all and knew that his life was over. This was how he would die. Drained, just like his parents.

Charles bit him, and it hurt so bad. Even worse, though, was the pressure of Charles sucking the blood from that vein. Each brutal draw sent that pain radiating through his body as if Charles was sapping every drop. He thought it hurt when Holly bit him, but nothing like the pain of Charles's bite.

Parker remembered starting to lose consciousness and being held up by Charles's strong arms. He wanted to struggle, to fight against him, but he couldn't. The pain started to fade as the world dimmed around him. Then, it felt like he died.

Except, here he was. Parker knew he wasn't dead. He was alive, awake, and hungry. Now that he'd been sitting there for a while, he realized he was really hungry and starting to have a hard time concentrating. Hungrier than he'd ever been in his life.

That's when Parker realized it was the hunger that had wakened him, and knew exactly what had happened. Charles hadn't killed him. He'd changed him. He was a vampire, now, and his hunger was starting to radiate through his body and dominate his every thought.

The door opened, and Charles walked in with an evil grin on his face. Parker glared back at him.

"Are you hungry, my new, little vampire?" Charles said. "You look like you're ready for your first taste of human blood."

"I'm hungry," Parker answered without intending to. He planned on not speaking to Charles at all, but the hunger made him answer.

"I thought you would be. Randall is bringing you food." Charles's face brightened as if he was giving Parker a gift. "Enjoy it."

Charles left. Parker didn't like that because the hunger kept growing and he didn't know who Randall was. Did Randall understand that Parker needed to feed? Did this Randall guy understand how the hunger was driving everything else from his mind?

Parker heard a commotion and a scream outside the door a moment before it opened. A vampire walked in shoving a human woman in front of him. Parker could smell the blood that ran slowly from the two small holes on her neck and knew it would taste so good. The hunger wanted it.

Her scent assaulted him and he leapt at the woman trapping her against the wall. He smelled her blood, and heard her heartbeat.

Parker felt fangs descend from his gums, and, somehow, he knew what to do. He plunged them in the woman's neck, right next to those other holes, while she screamed and he drank.

The vampire watched and laughed, the girl's screaming rang out through the room, and Parker continued drinking the most wonderful thing he'd ever tasted. He never wanted this to end.

The screaming stopped, and still Parker kept drawing blood from her vein. The easy flow of the blood slowed, and Parker had to draw harder. He supported the woman's entire weight between the wall and his body and had to lean in harder to keep her from falling. Then her heart stopped beating.

With the now silent heart, the blood was done flowing, and nothing was left for Parker to drink. He felt her lifeless body in his arms while he licked the last taste of her blood from her neck, his teeth, and his lips. Then he stepped back to let her fall to the floor.

"Excellent," Randall said quietly. "You rest while I feed. Then we'll dispose of her. Charles will be so proud." His voice was evil and sarcastic at the same time, and he didn't seem to be any more pleasant than Charles.

Parker went back to his cot but was not tired enough to lie down. He sat, leaned his back against the wall, and relished the feeling of not being hungry. He couldn't remember a greater feeling.

Inside, there was a part of him that was very satisfied and contented. He looked over at the body sprawled along the base of the wall and knew that was the cause of the contentment. That body and the taste of her blood that was still in his mouth.

He was finally a vampire. Not changed by Byron, which was what he'd always wanted, but changed. Now he knew the power of being able to claim and overcome his prey. He knew he had strength, speed, and heightened senses that made it possible to overpower any human.

Then he thought about Holly, and the time she'd attacked him. He'd always thought she would have been able to stop if Byron hadn't interfered. Could he have stopped drinking while that woman had any blood left in her body? Did he want to stop or wish he had stopped?

The door opened again and Randall came in. "Pick up that woman and follow me," he said.

Parker did as he was told, carrying her like a child. "Where are we going?"

"I need to show you how to get rid of her. The furnace works very nicely."

Randall led Parker to a door that opened onto what looked like a utility room of some kind. In the corner was a huge old furnace with the glow of a bright fire shining around its door.

Randall opened it. "Throw her in," he said.

Parker looked down at the cold, dead face of the woman he held in his arms. She felt like she weighed nothing, looked so small and helpless. Suddenly, this felt so wrong.

"So, you're training me?" he whispered, still staring at the woman.

"Yes."

"When will you teach me about control?" Parker turned his gaze to Randall.

"What do you mean by control?"

"How to stop feeding before she dies."

"Throw her in!" Randall shouted, scowling.

Parker placed her body in the flames as gently as possible and stood back to watch the flames surround her. When he finished feeding, he'd felt great. This, though, made him feel wrong.

Randall swung the door of the furnace closed, blocking Parker's view of the blackened, destroyed body. He grabbed Parker's upper arm and led him back to his room without a word.

"I'll tell Charles how you did," he said as he closed and locked the door. That statement sounded almost like a threat.

Time passed slowly as Parker sat alone in that room, but each passing minute helped him think more clearly. Unfortunately, most of those thoughts weren't pleasant ones.

At first, most of them had to do with the poor girl's dead face. She was lovely and really young, but Parker realized he hadn't noticed a thing about her until he was ready to put her in that furnace.

While feeding, she was prey. A simple food source to be devoured and disregarded. That's what the hunger had done to him. It made him transform a vital human being into a helpless, lifeless victim.

For the first time, Parker began to understand what Holly was talking about. It didn't matter how much she loved him, her hunger would have made him prey. Helpless, worthless, disposable prey. That's why she called it the beast, or the monster.

Parker thought of Byron who worked so hard against vampires like Charles. He owed Byron everything and wanted so much to make him proud. Killing that helpless woman would not have made him proud.

The more he thought about Byron and Holly, the more determined he became that he would not kill again. The next time, he would find the strength to stop feeding. He had to.

Just dozing off, he heard the door open again and Charles entered. Without saying a word, he grabbed Parker by the neck of his shirt and pulled him to his feet.

"Time to leave," Charles snarled into Parker's face. He let go of the shirt to grasp Parker's arm and half dragged him into a hallway and out a small door to a waiting car.

"Where are we going?" Parker asked.

"To meet a couple friends of yours." Charles gave him a nasty grin before dumping him in the back seat of the car. Randall was already in the driver's seat and Charles got in the front with him.

Parker looked around, but didn't recognize anything and didn't remember arriving at this run-down place. They passed a neighborhood drug store that had an Ohio State Block O in the window, so he figured he was in Columbus, but that was his only clue.

Randall turned down a street that seemed to have nothing but empty stores and a couple bars. Then he pulled to the sidewalk and Charles got out.

"What are we doing?" Parker asked, so confused. He couldn't figure out what Charles intended, or what he should expect to happen next.

"You'll find out," was all Randall would say.

Only a few minutes passed before Parker saw Charles walking back with a woman. She was dressed in a really short skirt with a skimpy top, had stringy blond hair falling down over half her face, and arms that were covered with tattoos.

Charles opened the back door and pushed her in next to Parker. "Thought you might like a snack," Charles said as he got back in the front seat.

Randall pulled away from the curb while Parker stared at the woman sitting next to him. She scooted closer to him, and he could smell the alcohol, cigarette smoke, and old sweat that surrounded her.

"The big guy says I'm all yours, so what'll it be, baby?" She put her hand on his chest and slid it up to caress his neck.

That was when Parker smelled her. He couldn't help but lean closer to her and inhale the scent of that tempting blood inside her. He heard it course through her veins as the beat of her heart rang through his ears. She was disgusting, but her blood would taste wonderful.

His gums tingled as his fangs began to descend and he pressed his face against her neck relishing that luscious scent. She was filthy, and Parker could smell the drugs in her blood, but he didn't care. He wrapped a hand around the back of her head to hold her in the right position. His other hand went around her waist so she couldn't get away. She giggled.

Just moments ago he hadn't felt hungry at all, but now? Now, he was ravenous. The beating of her heart, the smell of the blood flowing through her veins. Hunger was all he knew as his fangs plunged into her vein and he began to feed.

She screamed and struggled. She cried out for him to stop. Stop? Why would he want to stop? Her blood tasted so good, and he was so hungry. Her blood filled him and the beast inside rejoiced.

Stop? Something in the back of his mind said he should stop, but the hunger wouldn't consider it. That beast screamed for him to feed, to consume his prey. It couldn't be denied.

The hunger was everything and this blood satisfied it. This blood satisfied him, because he was the beast. Parker knew he was the predator, and this human was his prey. He devoured her because that's what he was designed to do.

He drank from her until she was a lifeless shell lying across his chest and no more blood would flow. He pushed her away and watched as her body crumpled half on the floor, half on the seat. Then he smiled as he licked his lips and teeth.

Parker looked up to realize they were parked along a river and he was alone. He didn't know where Charles and Randall might have gone, but figured he should get rid of that body.

He got out of the car, walked around to the other side, and grabbed her with one arm around her waist. Carrying her under his arm like a rag, he walked down to the river and threw her out to the middle. Wasn't it amazing that he was strong enough to easily throw a person that far?

He looked around and realized he was still in the city, but in an isolated area. He could see the lights of buildings nearby and smell the car exhaust from the highway on the other side of the river. Mostly, though, he could smell humans.

There were so many of them out there. No one had ever told him that he'd be able to smell humans like this. Their blood surrounded him, and he knew he could reach out and take that blood whenever he wanted. He had all the strength and power he needed to overcome and subdue that human prey, and they were completely helpless.

He was tempted to walk toward the human scents, but heard Charles and Randall walking back to the car, and he smelled them. It was so easy to distinguish vampire from human, and one vampire from another. He laughed at himself for once thinking that he could smell vampires when he was human. This was so different, so much more.

"You disposed of her?" Charles asked.

"Yes," Parker answered.

"How do you feel?"

Parker took a deep breath, raised his chin, and glared at Charles. "Strong," he finally answered.

Charles smiled. "Excellent! Get in the car."

They drove away with Parker still marveling at his vampire senses as he experienced the sights, sounds, and scents of the human city around him. Byron had never told him it would be like this. Maybe there were several things Byron had never told him.

Charles couldn't help feeling the satisfaction of how well things were going with Parker. He hadn't changed a human in many centuries because he hadn't been willing to follow the Assembly's rules. He'd never been willing to take it slow and train a young one to have control.

He felt like an artist whose masterpiece sat on the back seat behind him. His age and power made his vampire creation even stronger than others could create, and made that creation even more bloodthirsty. It was his power that Parker was feeling. Too bad he couldn't let him live very long to enjoy that power.

The whole point of all this was to make Byron suffer. Byron needed to watch helplessly as his son became bloodthirsty, and be just as helpless as he found his lifeless body. Then, he could watch the others close to him die other horrible deaths. The top of the list of those to die, the one Charles would most enjoy killing would be Holly.

Charles wasn't sure how Byron would proceed, but there was no doubt at all that he would show up at the cemetery. If he brought Holly and Luke, all the better. If not, he'd find Parker dead and Charles could continue on to the next step to kill Holly.

One step at a time. Step one had been Quinton, to show Byron the futility of searching for him. Step two had been accomplished with Clair's death and her help in taking Parker. Now, step three was in progress and Byron would see his world crumble around him until nothing was left except his own worthless life. Then

Charles would take that, too. Byron wouldn't be easy to kill. But with patience and his methodical plan, he'd succeed.

Charles looked at the young, bloodthirsty vampire sleeping in the back seat and couldn't help smiling again. One more feeding would be the safest plan, he thought. That way, if Byron could somehow save Parker's life, he'd never be able to turn him from bloodthirst, and the Assembly would be forced to execute him.

There was no way Byron could win this one. Parker would die either by Charles's hand or by the Assembly's law. Charles didn't care which. It was all working beautifully.

Randall pulled through the gate of the huge, old cemetery, and Parker woke as the car came to a stop.

"Where are we?"

"A cemetery. We'll spend the day here," Charles answered.

"You trying to prove the humans right about us?" Parker said sarcastically as he looked around.

Charles actually laughed. He was surprised at Parker's sense of humor. "Some friends will meet us here tonight."

"Your friends, or mine?"

"Yours, of course."

"Byron won't be happy that you changed me."

"I'm sure he won't. But, unlike others, I don't live to make Byron happy. Get inside the mausoleum. Randall will find someone to feed you."

"I'm not hungry." Parker wondered why he was being fed so often.

"You will be," Charles answered.

The mausoleum was cold, damp and dark. The walls were lined with plaques naming the people buried within the walls, but the floor space was empty and surprisingly small considering the size of the building. Of course, he realized, the walls were thick enough to hold the coffins. Parker thought it felt creepy, even to a vampire.

He looked around while Charles stepped outside to talk on his cell. More quickly than Parker expected, though, Randall and Charles came walking in with three women. Parker could smell cheap perfume and human blood. His hunger took notice.

"This place is awful creepy. It's gonna' cost you extra," one of them said. But Parker knew even before she said anything that they were other prostitutes they'd found somewhere on the street.

"Not a problem," Charles said as he took one woman's arm and led her toward Parker. "This one's for you," he said, grinning evilly into Parker's eyes.

Then he turned and took another one by the shoulders and slammed her back against the plaques on one of the walls. "Hey," she yelled. "No rough stuff." Charles sneered and showed her his fangs. Then she screamed.

Randall already had the other woman on the floor, but she started screaming, too, as he revealed his fangs and lunged at her, pretending to bite.

The women's screams sparked Parker's hunger, and his gaze fell on the woman Charles had pushed toward him. She was cringing in fear beating on the heavy door, trying to get out. The smell of that fear ignited his hunger even more. He threw himself at her, pinning her against the door.

Her arms were trapped between her body and the door as Parker's body pressed against her back and held her motionless. He reached around to her face and grasped her chin, pulling her head back to expose her neck. His face was buried in that space below her ear as he inhaled her scent and felt her blood pulsing against his lips.

She screamed, and he couldn't wait any longer. His fangs punctured her vein and he drank. He smelled the blood of the other two women mixed with the taste of hers, and the predator in him was so happy. He drew harder on her vein and quickly drained her, letting her collapse to the floor.

"Dump them somewhere, and get back to Thirst," Charles said to Randall. "Come back here right after nightfall so we're ready for him."

Randall gathered all three bodies in his arms and half dragged them out. Charles turned to Parker, who was still licking his lips. "Did you enjoy that?"

"Yes," Parker said, feeling the satisfaction of the beast inside him.

"Do you feel powerful?" Charles's voice was almost teasing, but that was exactly how Parker felt.

"Very."

"Let's see how powerful," Charles sneered as he walked slowly toward Parker. He grabbed his throat, lifting him from his feet, and threw him against the wall.

Parker recovered quickly and jumped back to his feet. He remembered how TJ had pushed him around in the woods that night. Well, he wasn't a helpless human now. He threw himself at Charles and attempted to tackle him to the ground.

Charles hardly moved from the hit. He laughed as he reached back and punched Parker in the jaw. Parker landed in the middle of the floor and Charles started kicking him. After several kicks, he grabbed his throat again and pulled him to his feet.

"We'll see how powerful you feel after you've lost half your blood and been exposed to the sun all day," Charles said as he held him only inches from his face.

Then he started beating Parker brutally. Charles's strength and speed made Parker's attempts to fight back completely useless. Once he was bleeding and barely conscious from the repeated punches and kicks, Charles picked him up, took him outside, and carried him up a ladder to the roof. Everything was ready there.

Charles had bolted the chains into the roof of the mausoleum over a week before. When he'd finished, he'd taken a minute to picture Parker held helpless and bleeding under those chains. Now it was time to make that vision a reality.

He wrapped the first chain around Parker's chest, and then moved to his thighs, his ankles, and finally his throat. Stretching Parker's arms out parallel to his shoulder's, Charles then chained his biceps and wrists.

Charles noticed that Parker's wounds had already begun to heal, which meant he would wake up soon, maybe too soon. Those three quick feedings would make him strong enough to heal quickly, but they were necessary. They insured that Parker would never find the control to overcome bloodthirst. If he lived long enough to even try.

The spring sun might not be strong enough to kill Parker unless he was adequately weakened. Charles also noticed clouds starting to roll through the pre-dawn sky and knew he'd have to make sure Parker was as weak as possible. Charles took out a dagger and slashed it across Parker's abdomen.

Parker groaned, barely conscious of what Charles was doing to him, as his blood flowed and pooled against his sides. That should ensure that the sun would inflict the debilitating, agonizing death that Charles had planned. The pain would wake Parker in plenty of time for him to realize he would soon be dead, and that pain would intensify as any exposed skin reddened and blistered.

Best of all in Charles mind, Parker should be long dead by the time Byron got there at midnight. If things went extremely well, Charles would have Holly and Luke, and Byron would be left to find Parker's bloody, burned body. All the result of a carefully executed plan.

Chapter 9

For the second day in a row, I hardly slept. Instead, I walked around Rule the Night, walked around my room, talked to Luke who was on duty through the day, but mostly I cried. The tears weren't constant, but they kept coming back no matter what I did.

I couldn't stop thinking about Parker. The worry about what Charles could be doing to him was almost debilitating, and I felt so miserable that I hadn't trusted him. Somehow, I had actually convinced myself that he had something going on with Clair. I was such a fool. I knew deep inside that Parker would never cheat on me.

Then I had to add on the worry about Chris and Lorna. Lorna was a powerful vampire trained in combat and perfectly capable of taking care of herself. But could she have any chance to win against Charles?

Chris was human. Weak, vulnerable to a vampire's mental control, and hardly aware of what dangers he faced. Lorna would do everything she could to protect him, but she may not be able to do enough. The whole thing made me so miserable and I felt so helpless.

Then I discovered that I could feel so much worse.

My phone rang. The display said it was from Parker. My heart leapt into my throat as I anticipated getting a message that said he was on his way home with Chris and Lorna. Safe and coming back to me.

It was a video message. I froze in the middle of my bedroom floor as I watched and realized what I was seeing.

I ran to Byron's suite. He and Crystal might have been sound asleep, but I was hysterical and had to get to him. I plunged through the door without even knocking and saw the two of them sitting on the couch staring at the phone Byron held in his hand.

Right behind me, TJ, Quinton, and Luke rushed headlong into the room. I knew we'd all gotten the same message when I saw their phones in their hands.

Crystal looked up at us, but Byron stared straight ahead with an expression on his face that made me think he was trying to keep his head from exploding. Was it anger, fear, shock, or all of the above? It had to be all of the above because that was what I was feeling. Mostly, it was deadly, cold rage.

"You all got it?" Byron finally asked. He was so horribly upset, his fangs showed and his voice was barely a whisper.

We all nodded at him.

"I will find him and kill him if it's the last thing I do," he yelled as he slammed his fist into the huge coffee table and smashed it into dozens of pieces. I got the idea he wasn't necessarily speaking to us. It was like he was announcing his intentions to the universe, or just had to scream out loud what he was feeling.

My tears started again and I realized my whole body was trembling. Quinton put his arm around my shoulders to offer some comfort, but he wasn't in much better shape than I was. None of us could wrap our minds around what we watched on that video. It was beyond what any of us could have imagined.

Charles had obviously sent it from Parker's phone. It showed Parker feeding, draining his victim, and dropping her lifeless body to the floor. There was a close-up of him licking his bloody lips and fangs as he watched her body slide down a wall. An arrogant expression of conquest and satisfaction grew on a face I barely knew. Not my sweet Parker anymore. Charles was letting us all know that he had changed Parker, and let him succumb to bloodthirst.

Our phones all beeped again as we stood there. I didn't want to look, but had to. I had to know.

The text said:

There might be time to save him, don't you think? Send me Holly and Luke as planned if you want him to have any chance. Charles

"What does he mean?" I gasped. With the shaking and crying, I could hardly recognize my own voice. "It's only been two days. Parker isn't really changed, is he?"

"Charles must have forced his change by feeding him too much vampire blood," Byron said

"Forced his change?"

"It's …" he started to answer me. Then his voice broke, and a tear ran down his cheek. I'd never seen Byron so out of control of his emotions, but I couldn't blame him.

"Holly," TJ said, taking over for Byron. "It's the way we used to change humans, all in one night. But we discovered that changing slowly helped avoid bloodthirst. The faster the change, the harder it is to learn control."

I couldn't believe my ears. Charles not only changed Parker, he changed him in a way that would make him bloodthirsty. My knees started to give out on me. Luckily, Quinton still had his arm around my shoulders and he caught me before I hit the floor.

Quinton walked me over to the couch and I immediately wrapped my arms around Byron, sobbing on his shoulder. I felt Byron's tears land on my neck.

"Can you save him?" I mumbled into Byron's chest. "I'll go to Charles."

"No! Charles sent this to entice me into giving up you and Luke tonight. Instead of sending you to the cemetery, I'm going directly to Thirst, at dusk. Charles won't live to see another day. I'll bring Parker back, Holly."

"I'll go with you," TJ said. His voice was so hard and determined.

"So will I," Quinton said a second later.

"And me," Luke added. "And don't forget Lorna's there. We can count on her."

I felt Byron move his head off my shoulder. He must have looked up at them. "Crystal, would you take care of Holly while we make some plans?"

"Byron, don't go without me!" I begged, almost hysterical.

"We're going there to attack. You're not strong enough or prepared adequately for that."

"What about Chris? He's completely helpless! Once Lorna joins you, they'll kill Chris." I couldn't control my crying or my voice. I was really close to losing it.

Byron rubbed those lines between his eyes again. "Chris ..." I think he'd forgotten about Chris for a second. Could I blame him, with so much on his mind? "Chris should be in the bar. You and Luke can go in as a couple and get him out right before the attack."

"Where does that leave me?" Luke asked.

"You take care of Holly and Chris. Once they're out, you join us, and we'll all move in."

I gave him a look, and he knew that I was going to say that I wanted to do more. "That's it, Holly. I won't take the chance of losing you. You need to take care of Chris, and we'll get Parker."

"Okay," I said quietly.

We spent the rest of the day making our plans. Besides the strategy for how to attack Charles, Byron put Crystal in charge of

Rule the Night with Anthony and the guards from the Assembly filling in for TJ, Quinton and Luke.

The Assembly guards all wanted to be part of the strike against Thirst, but someone had to make sure Rule the Night was secure. We were full of clients, so we couldn't just close. Besides, closing would give Charles a huge hint that we might be moving against him. Byron wouldn't do anything that might warn Charles.

Byron called Constance to tell her of our plans, and we found out that Constance already had two undercover guards at Thirst, watching for Charles. She'd get word to them and they'd join Byron as soon as the attack started.

By late afternoon, we were ready to go. Making our move right after dark would catch Charles off guard the most, and it would mean that the fewest number of humans would be in the bar. None of us were willing to endanger any more humans than necessary, and a vampire battle wasn't something that humans needed to see. Or something that many would survive.

The five of us climbed into the big SUV with the specially tinted windows that would protect us from the sun until it finally set. I was too young for even those windows to really protect me, so I got wrapped up in a blanket.

Quinton had strapped daggers with sheaths around my arm and waist, but the rest of them carried many more weapons including what TJ called a garrote. It was a thin wire with handles at the ends and was an ancient weapon used to strangle someone. It looked to me like a tiny jump rope, but what did I know about methods of killing?

"Why not guns?" I'd asked TJ.

"Bullets just don't make big enough wounds unless you can blow out some brains. Knives can slash major arteries to cause the rapid blood loss that will kill. Of course snapping the neck to kill the brain stem works best."

Kind of a How to Kill a Vampire 101 type answer, but it was what I needed to know. Maybe I should have sent a lot of knives with Chris rather than the gun. I didn't know how I was going to deal with this. What if things went wrong?

I was just glad we were finally on the way. It was torment to think of what Parker had gone through. I'd seen the video Charles sent, but still couldn't really get my head around the fact that Parker was now a vampire. A bloodthirsty vampire.

A little part of me kept thinking that it just couldn't be true. Maybe Charles had faked the video somehow to lure Byron into doing just what we were on our way to do. Maybe Parker was actually fine and would be home and his normal self by morning. Maybe I was just lying to myself with that wishful thinking, but I couldn't help it.

* * *

Chris woke up about 2:00 in the afternoon to a knock on the door. Lorna was soundly sleeping right through the gentle, but insistent, rapping sound. He pulled on his jeans and held Parker's gun behind his back before opening the door a few inches. It was one of the bartenders standing in the hall with an anxious look on his face.

"I have to talk to you and Lorna," he said so quietly Chris had a little trouble hearing him.

"Who are you?" Chris answered. He wasn't going to let a strange vampire who worked for Charles into their room without some explanation.

"I'm Carson. I know you're Chris, Holly's brother," he said. "Lorna knows me. Just wake her before someone finds me here." He was getting a little irritated.

Chris wasn't going to turn his back on this guy to wake Lorna. "Wait in the hall," he said as he closed the door in the vampire's face. He was acting as fearless as he could, but knew this vampire could easily push him aside or just control his mind to get in.

"Lorna," Chris called as he shook her shoulder. It took several shakes to get her to respond and open her eyes. "One of the bartenders is at the door. His name's Carson and says he needs to talk to us."

Lorna jumped out of bed and grabbed her robe as she dashed to the door. "He's a friend," she said as she passed Chris.

Not only did she let the vampire in, the two of them hugged and gave each other one of those European kisses – kissing next to each of the other person's cheeks. Obviously, he was a friend.

"Chris," she said, "Carson is from the Assembly. We've known each other for centuries. Carson, this is Chris."

"Sorry to catch you by surprise like this," Carson said as he shook hands with Chris, "but I just got a message from Constance."

Chris had to stop and think about who Constance was but finally remembered she was the one Byron talked to about the whole plan of sending him and Lorna to Thirst. She was the head of that group they called the Assembly, but Chris really didn't know if that made her like a president, a judge, or a cop.

"Byron's attacking Thirst tonight, and you two need to be ready."

"What happened?" Lorna asked.

"Did they get Holly?" Chris asked with alarm at the same time. They both knew that something was going on if Byron was changing his plans so drastically.

"It's something with Parker. I don't know what, but I'm guessing that Byron must have found out for sure that Charles is keeping him here. They're going to move in right after dark. You two need to be in the bar as soon as it opens. Someone will come in to take you out," he nodded toward Chris, "before Byron strikes."

"Take me out?"

"They want you out of it. Once Lorna joins Byron, he's afraid Charles will target you."

"Is Holly with them?" Chris couldn't bear the thought of Holly fighting. He knew that she was a powerful, deadly vampire like the rest of them, but still couldn't see her as anything but his little sister.

"I don't know for sure but I doubt it. Byron wouldn't put someone as young as she is in the middle of this."

"Chris," Lorna said, "we have to trust Byron. He wouldn't put Holly in danger." Chris just looked at Lorna without saying anything, but his expression showed that he wasn't completely convinced of that.

"I have to go," Carson said. "Besides me, one of the waitresses, Marla, is also from the Assembly. She'll join us when things get started."

Chris and Lorna had a million things to talk about once Carson left, but most of it was speculation. Lorna felt a responsibility for making sure Chris knew what to do once things got going, so she went through several "what-if" scenarios. They all ended the same way, though. Chris had to get out and keep himself safe no matter what happened.

That didn't make Chris extremely happy. He came here to help, and didn't like the idea of doing nothing except protecting himself. If Holly was involved, he needed to make sure she was safe. They both wished they knew more details of Byron's plan, but all they could really do was guess.

Eventually, they had to get ready to face whatever would happen in the bar once it opened. Lorna made sure Chris had the gun strapped on correctly, carefully covered by a light jacket, before strapping several different weapons on herself. She had knife sheaths on both forearms and at her right ankle as well as a heavy lead bar in her pocket.

"What's that for?" Chris asked. He'd been around enough to have seen more hand-to-hand weapons than he really needed to know, but this was a new one to him.

Lorna grinned. "My hand's not as big and I'm not as strong as many males. Holding this in my fist makes my punches much more effective than they'd be with my bare hand."

"Tricky," he grinned. "Is that how you handle all those guys trying to get in the bar without ID's?"

"I wouldn't use this on a human. With humans, it's all me." She gave him a sexy grin as she gazed into his eyes.

"Lorna, you're going to be okay through all this, right?" Chris couldn't stand the thought that she might be hurt or killed.

"Of course I am," Lorna said as she reached up and hugged him. They held on to each other.

"I care a lot about you, you know?" Chris whispered against her neck.

"I know ... and I feel the same way about you."

Getting to the bar a few minutes later, they sat at the small table like they had the night before and tried to act like they were looking forward to a pleasant evening of socializing and dancing.

Carson was behind the bar and a waitress come over to take their order.

"Hi," she smiled. "I'm Marla," she said, letting them know she was on their side. "What can I get you?"

Everything seemed to be set, and Chris was trying to hide his nerves without much success.

Lorna leaned toward him. "I can smell your fear," she whispered. "Would it help if I controlled it for you?"

"I just need to get my mind off it," he said. Then he leaned closer and kissed her. "That helped," he smiled before wrapping his arms around her and kissing her again.

"Very resourceful," she smiled back.

"Lorna?" a familiar voice said over her shoulder.

"Oh, my," she said reaching for Luke's hand without using his name. "What brings you to the states?"

"Christine and I are just exploring," Luke said, indicating the woman with him. Chris couldn't help his smile as he saw it was Holly. "And your companion?"

"This is Chris, my human lover," Lorna said. Chris hadn't gotten used to being called that. It seemed somehow crude, but that was the correct vampire term for his relationship with Lorna, especially since she'd now fed from him.

Lorna, though, kept thinking about the huge chance Luke and Holly were taking. Charles wanted both of them, and several of his employees might recognize them at any time. They needed to get out of Thirst fast.

"Hello, Chris, I'm James," Luke said. Now everyone knew what fake names Luke and Holly were using.

No matter what names they gave, or how happy he was to see her, Chris really didn't like the idea of Holly being there. He didn't join in the small talk that went on for several minutes because he was a little afraid of saying something wrong, like calling Holly by her real name.

"What do you think, Chris?" Lorna asked him.

"Uh, I'm sorry?" he answered. He hadn't been listening to the conversation at all. Instead, he'd been looking around, worrying as he realized that someone could recognize Holly or Luke.

"James and Christine are going to some art galleries and want us to join them. Do you want to go?"

For a second, Chris didn't know how to answer her but he soon realized that this was the excuse for them all to leave. "Sure, that's great," he finally said.

The four of them walked to the front door and smiled at the guards as they left. Waiting for the valet seemed to take forever and they waited in silence.

"Here he comes," Lorna said as the car finally came into view. "Where to?" she asked Luke as she started to pull away.

"Over there," Luke said, pointing into the dark.

They drove a short distance to another abandoned warehouse and pulled behind to find Byron, TJ and Quinton waiting. They only had a minute to greet each other, and then say goodbye. Chris hated letting Lorna go.

Chris and Holly watched as everyone else jogged back toward Thirst. This was it. Holly knew that Byron would succeed in getting Parker back, or die in the attempt. But she also had faith in Byron and had to believe that their plan would work. Before the night was over, Parker would be safe and Charles would be dead. She had to believe that.

As they started around the building toward the other car, a voice said from the darkness, "We meet again, Holly." Holly knew instantly that it was Noel.

"Go!" she screamed at Chris.

At the same instant, Holly pulled a knife from her wrist sheath and charged headlong at the vampire who was strolling slowly toward them.

No way could Chris run away and leave Holly. He drew his gun, but knew he couldn't shoot accurately enough to avoid hitting her, so he ran to get closer. The vampires moved so fast, Chris could hardly keep track of what happened, but by the time he got close to them, the results were not good.

The guy was bleeding from his chest, but had Holly in a neck hold with her knife poised to slice her throat.

"I wouldn't try anything foolish, little human," he said with an evil grin. The wound from Holly's knife didn't seem to affect him at all.

The whole thing seemed so unreal to Chris. He was standing there pointing a gun he barely knew how to use at Holly and this monster who had a knife at her throat. What could he do? What move wouldn't be stupid?

"Noel," Holly was saying, "he's not involved in anything, just Lorna's lover. Let him go."

"Not your dinner?" he asked sarcastically. "I thought we could share a meal like old friends. Wouldn't that be nice, Holly?"

"He's not mine," she said.

"Lorna's feeding with Randall," Chris said. "Holly, Lorna won't like this." Chris had finally started thinking through how to play this situation. This guy wouldn't have any way to know that Byron was attacking. Maybe he'd be more afraid of Lorna than Holly.

"With Randall?" Noel almost laughed. "So, Holly, she got you to watch her little pet while she found other entertainment. Who is this Lorna?"

"Just a friend of mine," Holly answered. She knew what Chris was thinking, but he didn't know her history with Noel and how he'd love nothing more than to kill her or take her to Charles. The longer she could keep him here, though, meant one less vampire fighting against Byron.

"Does Byron know you have a friend who enjoys bloodthirst? Or … Is she working for Byron?" Noel was figuring out that it really didn't make any sense for Holly to be at Thirst, so something must be going on. "What are you really doing here?"

Through all the discussion, Holly felt Noel's grip relax slightly and the knife move a fraction of an inch away from her skin. He was distracted and hadn't even attempted to control her arms. Holly waited for her chance to get to the second knife she had strapped to her waist.

"Who's Byron?" Chris asked. Holly gave him a tiny grin that she knew Noel couldn't see. Good thinking, Chris.

"Don't worry about him," Holly answered.

"Look," Chris said like he was getting irritated. "Lorna's going to be mad as hell. She wanted me to show you a good time, but she won't want me involved in whatever you have going with this guy. I'm going back to Thirst. You two do … whatever."

As Chris talked, Holly felt Noel relax even more. The knife moved farther from her neck. He was enjoying listening to the human who thought he had something to say about the situation. Then Noel laughed at Chris.

She felt his grip loosen and knew that was what she'd been waiting for. She pulled the knife out gently with her right hand, spun suddenly to the left, and plunged it deeply into Noel's neck. Directly into the jugular.

Chris gasped and jumped back a foot as the blood spurted over all three of them. Noel dropped to his knees and grabbed at the knife sticking out of his neck to try to stop the bleeding. His face was at Holly's waist as she glared down at him and put her hands on either side of his head.

"You deserve to suffer more than this," she said quietly as she snapped his neck.

Chris almost fainted. His little sister had just killed some guy by slitting his throat and casually snapping his neck. He'd never seen anyone die, let alone die like that.

"Holly," he whispered. His knees were wobbling and he thought he might faint after all.

"I'm sorry, Chris." She grabbed him around the waist to steady him. "You didn't need to see that, but he's the one that helped Charles escape from Nibble. He's tortured and killed so many humans. I couldn't let him live."

"He was bloodthirsty?" Chris asked.

"Yes. And he would have killed both of us without a second thought. I think the only reason he didn't was that Charles wants me captured."

"I know you had to do it. I just didn't expect it, you know?" He still gazed down at the dead vampire, looking confused and still scared.

"Yeah. You were great, though. I wouldn't have been able to get to my knife if you hadn't distracted him like that."

"Maybe we're a pretty good team, huh?" He tried to keep it light, but the shock of the whole thing still showed on his face.

"We always were fighting Mom and Dad," Holly smiled.

"Let's get out of here," Chris said, putting his arm around Holly's shoulders. "Doesn't all this blood bother you?" They were both covered with it and Chris started to think about how soon he could get in a shower.

"Vampire blood doesn't tempt us, only human blood." They started walking back to the car still holding on to each other.

"I want you to know that I asked Lorna to bite me," Chris said quietly as they walked.

"Did she?"

"This morning."

"Are you okay? I mean … were you scared?"

"Not with Lorna," Chris smiled. "She'd never hurt me."

"Chris, I'm sorry all this has been thrown on you. I should have told you sooner."

"Na," he squeezed her a little, shaking his head. "I would have been scared shitless if I hadn't gotten to know everyone first. It's all good."

They got back to the car and Chris got in the driver's seat. "Don't stop until you get to Rule the Night, and …" Holly was saying when Chris interrupted.

"Oh, no! You're not sending me back while you stay. The only reason I was leaving was to get you home." His eyes showed his fear and growing anger. "Get in the car."

"I can't walk away and leave them."

"Get in the damn car, Holly!" Chris shouted.

Holly cringed and whispered, "Have you any idea how much you just sounded like Dad?"

Chris lowered his head and rubbed his eyes. "Oh, God. I never wanted to be anything like him." He hesitated, then added. "Holly, I can't stand the thought of you fighting in there and maybe getting hurt."

"I think I showed you I can take care of myself. I have to, Chris. I just have to." Her eyes were so sad and determined.

"Then I'm going with you, and I'll shoot anyone that touches you. Seriously, I don't like the idea of running away, either."

Holly gazed at him trying to think of a way to talk him into leaving.

"Look," Chris said. "We both have people in there that we … love. We can't leave them."

"You love her?"

"Falling fast."

"Damn it," Holly sighed. "Then, let's go."

Chapter 10

As soon as they could see no customers in the parking lot, Byron and TJ strolled to the front door from the dark street like any two guys heading for a bar. The guards nodded a greeting when their scents identified them as two powerful vampires.

"Do you have a reservation, sir?" one guard asked Byron, recognizing him as the older, more powerful one.

"Believe me, we're not expected."

With that, he and TJ each grabbed the head of a guard and snapped their necks. Those two guys never even saw it coming. A split second later, TJ jumped up and punched out the overhead light, leaving the whole area in darkness. That was the signal for Quinton, Luke, and Lorna to join them.

The five of them walked into Thirst calmly and looked around. There weren't many customers in the bar, yet. It was just too early. But there was still an assortment of vampires and a few humans.

They knew there was at least one guard at the back door, several employees would be in different positions in the bar, and some of the clients would fight with Charles.

Those elements were the weakest part of their plan because they couldn't know how many enemies they would have to face. But they also knew that there were two Assembly spies that would join them once the fighting started.

They spread out to cover as much area as possible and to keep most of the vampires within sight. Byron caught Carson and Marla's eyes as they moved into position. Carson cut the music

CD that entertained the customers until the band came in about 10:00.

The other bartender, that wasn't from the Assembly, pushed the button that activated the silent alarm in Randall's office. Randall saw the alarm light and turned on the monitor that gave him access to the cameras in the bar area. He recognized Byron immediately and knew exactly what was about to happen.

Then he saw Quinton, Luke, and Lorna. Lorna, the one he and Charles both thought would be joining them in the morning. She was a spy. A good one, he had to admit.

Randall smiled because he knew them all. Then he smiled more broadly thinking about how proud Charles would be when he heard they were all dead. Except Byron. He'd save Byron for Charles to kill himself.

"Excuse me, ladies and gentlemen," Byron said as Randall watched them from the office. "Stay where you are until you're told to leave. Those of you dancing, find a seat. Now."

Luke, Lorna, and Quinton moved through the humans. They told them to leave, and removed their memories of being at Thirst. The vampires didn't know what was going on, but they knew it was something big. This was not normal at any sanctuary. They waited and watched.

Once the humans were gone, Byron announced, "I'm looking for Charles, Noel and Randall. As soon as they come to the bar, the rest of you may leave."

Byron knew the security cameras were sure to have identified them by now, and was sure Charles would be in the office plotting an attack, but he was not about to waste the lives of any innocent vampires that happened to be in the bar.

If some of the guilty escaped, so be it. This was about getting Parker back. The Assembly could worry about executing those who came here for bloodthirst. Byron's only concern right now was facing Charles and saving Parker. There was no way he could consider that Parker might already be dead.

Randall had woken two daytime guards who slept through most of the night and sent them outside to circle around to the front door, assuming the guards who'd been on duty there were dead. The daytime guards would attack Byron from behind while he and the back door guard would attack from the office hallway. Between the four of them, clients that would join in the fight, and the employees already in the bar, there should be no problem defeating Byron.

After Byron asked for Charles and Randall, there was silence. He'd hoped that at least a few vampires would claim no knowledge of them and ask to leave, but over a dozen sat there staring at him. Some of them were very young, though, and would be easy to kill, but Byron still wanted to avoid unnecessary killing if possible.

"Charles kidnapped my human, and I'm willing to kill to get him back. This is your last chance to leave."

No one moved or spoke. Obviously, they all knew enough to be very afraid of crossing Charles, or hoped to avoid trouble by not drawing attention to themselves. No one, though, would get through this night without being on one side or the other.

"Attack!" a booming voice yelled as the door from the office hallway flew open.

The voice reverberated through the bar, and two more guards dashed through the front door. Byron smelled them coming from behind before they could get to him. He spun and caught one with a kick to the gut that threw the guard against the wall and doubled him over. With two steps, Byron was on him and snapped his neck.

He looked to his right for the second one and saw him dead at TJ's feet. TJ was already moving on to one of the clients that was charging toward them. Quickly surveying the room, Byron saw that Carson had just killed the other bartender, and Marla was engaged in serious hand-to-hand with another client.

Randall was taking note of the situation in the room as Byron had been, and their eyes met. They flew toward each other. The impact was tremendous, but they both stayed on their feet. Byron slashed his dagger at Randall's throat, but Randall stepped away just in time to avoid a debilitating wound.

Randall attacked Byron, but aimed for his body instead of his throat, which convinced Byron that Randall was not attempting to kill. He wanted to wound him and take him to Charles.

"Where is Charles?" Byron asked as they parried and dodge each other's attacks.

Randall didn't answer.

"Is he afraid to face me?" Byron tried again.

Not getting an answer, Byron swung out with his right leg and caught Randall in the knee. The sound of crunching bone as Randall screamed and fell made it very obvious that the knee was crushed.

Byron dragged him to the wall to get out of the middle of the fight. Looking around again, things were not going well. Almost every one of his guards was fighting off two of Charles's supporters. Lorna was bleeding from two different knife wounds and Luke's nose was obviously broken.

TJ was holding his own and dropped one vampire as Byron watched. Quinton, though, was in trouble. Three vampires surrounded him and were getting him trapped against the bar.

Byron was torn between questioning Randall and helping Quinton when he saw the front door open again. The thought that

Charles or more of his followers had arrived caused him to realize that his attempt to rescue Parker may be failing. But the new arrivals weren't with Charles.

A shot rang out and one of Quinton's attackers fell. Before Byron could react, Holly was fighting next to Luke, and Chris pressed the gun against another vampire's temple and pulled the trigger again.

Slamming his fist into Randall's jaw to knock him out, Byron headed back into the fight. Another shot. Now three vampire's brains and blood were splattered around the bar. Chris was covered with it.

Byron ran to Holly and killed the vampire attacking her. Holly smiled up at him and turned to look for another. Byron grabbed her arm and pulled her toward the corner. Lorna stepped up to battle the one Holly was about to face.

Three very young vampires were cringing there, trying to stay away from the fighting.

"Holly, guard these three," he said. "Kill any one of them that tries to join the fighting."

Holly thought Byron was going to make her leave, so she was relieved that he'd given her a specific way to help. She could scent that one of the three was really young, probably just a month or so. What were they doing here?

She made them sit on the floor with their backs against one wall and held her knife on them. Being at a corner, she could stand with her back to the perpendicular wall and watch for anyone who might try to attack her from behind.

Byron looked back at her and was happy that she got herself in a strategic position. He heard another shot and saw more blood splatter. Chris had killed another vampire. He couldn't believe that a human who'd only learned about them days ago was handling this so well.

Holly and Chris's arrival had made an incredible difference. The tables were now turned and the fighting was slowing. It was now two of Byron's people against every one of Charles's vampires, and they were all starting to surrender.

The room grew quiet. Byron was relieved to see all his people had survived even though most were badly bruised and bleeding. Chris, though, stood over Carson's sprawled body. His neck was horribly twisted. Next to him was the bloody remains of the vampire who'd killed him. Chris's last shot had been too late to save Carson.

They made the four who surrendered move to the corner with the young ones, and Lorna and Luke took over guarding them. Holly went to Chris and put her arms around him.

"You were so brave!" she gasped.

"I was scared to death," he whispered back as they hugged.

Byron walked over and shook his hand. "Thank you, Chris. I'm very impressed."

Then Byron, TJ, and Quinton went over to Randall, pulled him to his feet, and slapped his face until he woke up. They needed some answers.

"Where are Charles and Parker?" Byron asked.

"I have no idea," Randall answered with a smug arrogance showing on his face.

Byron backhanded him hard enough that he slid down the wall he was leaning against. TJ pulled him back to his feet and slammed him against the wall.

"You're going to die one way or another," Byron said. He wasn't yelling, but his voice was so forceful that everyone in the bar could hear every word. "So do you want to die now or after you've had the pleasure of telling me how much you and Charles have made Parker suffer?"

All those who knew Parker and what Charles was capable of cringed. None of them wanted to hear about the atrocities that Parker must have suffered.

Randall smiled evilly. "You've got a point, old friend. I'm sure you got the video. That was just his first feeding. He's enjoyed draining two other women since then. But what he enjoyed the most was when Charles and I took him to the mausoleum last night and fed with him. The screams and spilled blood of three different women … imagine how luscious that was. Parker couldn't get enough of it. The look on his face when he fed while watching the two of us should make any father proud."

A wave of anger spread through the room as Byron glared at Randall. He slowly put his hand around Randall's throat and started to squeeze. Breathing wasn't an issue, but pain sure was as Byron tightened his grip. The look on Randall's face was horrible. He would have been screaming if he'd been able to force air through his vocal chords.

Byron just stared in Randall's eyes. Everyone could tell his grip tightened like a vise from the way Randall struggled and clutched at Byron's wrist. Every muscle, tendon, and blood vessel must have been crushed from the force of Byron's bare hand. Then Byron lifted him a foot off the floor.

No one moved, no one spoke, as they watched Byron hold the struggling, flailing Randall in the air, while Byron seemed to be completely relaxed. Only TJ had any idea Byron was that strong.

Finally, Byron spoke. "Hell is too good for you," he said quietly. Then he simply bent his wrist to the side and snapped Randall's neck. The crunching sound of the bones breaking seemed to be as loud as Chris's gunshots.

Randall's body thumped to the floor, and Byron turned his back and walked over to the vampires who had surrendered. They had all watched Byron kill Randall and were terrified.

"Luke, write down their names and whether or not they fought for Charles. Then show them out." Byron said. He looked at the young ones sitting against the wall, cringing. "The Assembly will want to question you about your presence here. Expect to hear from them."

* * *

We'd planned the whole invasion of Thirst to get Parker back, but now knew that Charles had already taken him to the cemetery. Charles would be waiting for Luke and me to show up at midnight and turn ourselves over in exchange for Parker.

Did that mean Charles was going to let Parker stroll out of there to go home with Byron? I couldn't imagine him doing that. We all knew that Charles was not one to keep his word.

Most likely, Charles had some plan to kill us all. That's what he really wanted. All of us dead, but especially Byron. I would be really surprised if Byron wasn't thinking the exact same thing.

I felt a strange kind of calm sitting there looking at Byron and waiting. But maybe I wasn't calm, maybe I was numb. My emotions had been so wired for the last several days that I began to think they'd all shut down.

"I've been thinking about how we go to the cemetery tonight," Byron started. "If we approach in force, Charles could easily kill Parker and escape. It's too dangerous to send Holly and Luke. So, the best thing is for me to go alone."

"Alone …" TJ said. "No backup, no support?"

"Alone!" Byron declared. "But not without backup. All of you will surround the mausoleum and come to my aid if necessary."

"He could have a small army in there with him," Quinton said.

"I suspect that most of his army is now dead at our feet," Byron answered looking around the room. "He probably only has Noel with him, and Randall would have taken others to the cemetery closer to midnight."

"I killed Noel out in the parking lot," I said quietly. They all stared at me like they'd forgotten I was there. "With Chris's help."

"You two are full of surprises," Byron said, looking dumbfounded. "I'll want to hear about that when we have more time."

"Byron," I said, "wouldn't Charles be more likely to talk if Luke and I went with you? If you're alone, he may not tell you anything about Parker."

"You're right, he might be more likely to talk," Byron said quietly, "but I won't take that risk with you. I'm the only one powerful enough to face Charles, so my decision is made."

When Byron used that tone of voice, we all knew that the discussion was over. It's not like he was mad. He was determined and he wouldn't be convinced to change his mind.

"What do you want us to do with these bodies?" TJ asked.

"We'll burn the building and let the sunlight take any remains in the morning. I don't want any trace left of the bodies or this place."

I wanted to go to Parker right away and I'm sure Byron did, too, but we had to cover our tracks. There would be a lot of problems if the cops found the bodies we left scattered around.

Quinton and I went out to the trees where we'd left Noel so we could put him inside to burn with the others. Lorna and Chris went downstairs to get the stuff they left in their room. TJ and Luke followed Marla to search the office and basement areas just in case anyone was left. Byron called Constance to let her know what we were doing and to report that Carson had died.

All these details kept us from Parker, but couldn't be helped. One thing I was very grateful for was that Byron was not going to wait for midnight to face Charles. We'd be leaving for the cemetery as soon as everything was cleaned up here. Couldn't be soon enough as far as I was concerned.

Finally, we stood in the parking lot watching Thirst burn. In that neighborhood, it would be a while before anyone called 911, but we needed to stay long enough to make sure any evidence of us being there was destroyed. Once the flames were consuming the whole building, we left Marla to keep an eye on things and deal with the fire department that would eventually show up. As soon as the sun rose, all trace of any bodies would be gone.

Chapter 11

We parked several blocks from the cemetery so we could sneak up on the mausoleum without Charles knowing what was going on. We'd hide from him until Byron needed us, but I knew that Byron hoped to not call us in at all.

We hadn't talked about what Byron was going to do, but we all knew, anyway. He was going to kill Charles just like he'd killed Randall.

My attitude about killing had changed quite a bit in the last six months. I'm sure becoming a vampire had a lot to do with it, but it was more than that. I'd been attacked by Colton and Leslie, I attacked Parker, and I'd seen the torture and killing that had gone on at Nibble.

I knew deep in my heart that some things had to be stopped and bloodthirst was one of them. I couldn't stop all the sick people who killed for money or power, abused and neglected their children, or thought it was fun to make others suffer, but I could stop some vampires who thought they had a right to kill humans.

That's why I didn't feel bad about killing Noel, even though I did feel bad that I had to do it in front of Chris. Noel was as guilty as Charles, Armand and Randall, and he'd needed to die just like them. Anyone who chose bloodthirst deserved to die.

The whole neighborhood surrounding the cemetery was silent, and we contributed no sound at all as we passed by. Chris and Lorna walked together, but I moved up to his other side and took his hand. I was a little scared of what could happen when we got to the mausoleum, but mainly I was weary, and needed comfort.

Chris let go of my hand and slid that arm around my shoulder. He knew exactly what I needed, probably because he felt the same way. I reached my arm around his waist and we continued down the street with Lorna holding his other hand and watching over both of us.

Once we were on the grass of the cemetery and close enough that Charles would soon be able to smell us coming, we stopped. TJ and Luke went to the right to cover the far side of the mausoleum while the rest of us went to the left to cover the back and closer side. Byron walked straight ahead toward the entrance.

We were all looking, sniffing, and listening for hints of any other vampires, but got nothing. If Charles had anyone with him, they were inside or even farther away than we were. It was hard to believe that he was alone, but Byron thought we might have done away with all his supporters and guards when we attacked Thirst. I hoped he was right.

Now, all we could do was wait. Wait for Byron to return with Parker, hopefully. Most likely, though, we were waiting for a call to move in and help defeat Charles. We weren't positive that Parker was here or if he was still alive. That was what scared me the most.

* * *

Byron approached the mausoleum with all his senses on high alert. One-on-one, he knew he could handle Charles, but not as easily as he'd taken care of Randall. The most important thing, though, was getting an indication of Parker. If Parker wasn't here, it was very unlikely that Charles could be forced to tell where he was being held.

Finally, he was close enough to smell Charles's presence, which meant Charles also knew that Byron was approaching. Byron stood about ten feet from the door and called to Charles. He got no answer.

"I know you're there, Charles. There is no point hiding. Open the door, or I'll come through it."

Byron spoke forcefully, but he felt almost defeated. He could smell Parker, but the scent wasn't comforting. No longer the human scent Byron was so accustomed to, but unmistakably vampire. Byron had held a faint hope that the video had been faked even though he knew that changing Parker would be exactly the kind of thing Charles would do.

More disturbing, though, was that the scent was faint and accompanied by the scent of dried blood. Dried vampire blood. It was possible that Parker was still alive, but Byron couldn't be sure. Charles had probably beaten him, possibly several times. It was an old torture technique to beat a vampire until unconscious, wait for them to heal, and start the beatings again.

Byron's temper was ready to flair as he thought about what Parker might have suffered at Charles's hands. He had to force himself to calm down. Charles was not only strong, but very intelligent. Byron would have to be the same and not let his rage take over. Whatever Charles had done, though, it was time for the stand-off to end.

Byron ran toward the door shoulder first slamming through it with little effort. He sprang into the empty space as the door crashed to the floor and glared at Charles who was leaning against the wall with his arms folded across his chest. He was grinning evilly.

"Give me Parker," Byron said with his voice showing all the anger inside him.

"Give me Holly and Luke," Charles shrugged.

Byron had enough. He knew Parker was close and injured, possibly dying, which meant he needed to get to him fast. The sooner Charles was out of the way, the better.

Within the blink of an eye, Byron had gone from standing by the destroyed door to grasping Charles around the neck with both hands. Charles was better at handling the pain than Randall had been and was better at defending himself.

Instead of trying to get Byron's hands off his neck, Charles pulled a knife from his waist sheath and attempted to stab Byron in the back.

Byron, though, knew Charles's skills and expected something like that from him. He let go with one hand, blocked the knife, knocked it from Charles's hand, and sent it skidding across the floor.

They were very evenly matched, and the blows started flying. Any human watching would have seen little more than a blur as they punched, kicked, and blocked each other. At one point Charles landed a lucky punch on Byron's nose and the blood started flowing.

Charles reached out for Byron's neck. Byron recognized what Charles was trying to do and stepped back slightly so Charles stretched farther than he'd planned and ended up locking his elbow in place. Byron saw the chance he was waiting for and struck the elbow from the side with his forearm. The joint snapped, and Charles's arm hung uselessly at his side.

Byron now had the advantage, but Charles wasn't beaten, yet. They continued the merciless blows and kicks, slamming each other against the plaques marking where human bodies filled the walls. If one fell, he got instantly back on his feet and continued the battle.

* * *

TJ couldn't stand the waiting and wondering what was happening in that mausoleum. He hadn't liked the idea of Byron going in alone from the beginning. There were too many ways it could all go wrong.

The biggest worry on his mind, though, since Byron left them, was the possibility that Charles could beat Byron. No fight was a sure thing, and if Charles won, he would probably take off with Parker, and none of them would have any idea he'd left.

He hated that he was disregarding Byron's orders, but he couldn't stand around doing nothing any longer.

"Luke, I'm going in," he said.

"Good. I've been wanting to, but figured I wouldn't be much help."

"Tell the others after I've gone."

TJ crept forward. Charles and Byron would both know he was near as he got close enough for them to catch his scent, but TJ was more concerned about what he was smelling. Byron's blood. Not much, but he was bleeding.

He heard their blows as he got closer and knew the fight was still on, and even though Byron was bleeding, it wasn't a serious injury. Then he stopped as he recognized the new scent wafting through the night air. Parker. Seriously injured and very weak.

TJ had intended going in to help Byron, but decided at the last minute to look around and see if he could find anything that would give them a hint about Parker. Byron would also know from Parker's scent that he was near death. If the fight with Charles was still going on, then Byron hadn't been able to get to Parker to help him.

He circled around the mausoleum checking for another entrance. All the while he listened to the battle going on inside while trying to get closer to where Parker was being held, but neither the sounds nor the scents changed. It made sense that the fight was going on in the middle of the mausoleum, but it seemed that Parker was being held in the same place.

Could Byron and Charles be fighting around Parker? Maybe Parker was unconscious, lying in the middle of the floor, while Byron struggled to get the upper hand. That didn't make sense to TJ. There just couldn't be that much space in there. TJ could hear that they were flying against walls and charging each other across the floor. Parker couldn't be in the center of that.

Maybe a basement? There was no reason for a basement in a mausoleum, but TJ continued around the building figuring he'd have to go in to find a basement entrance. Then he spotted a ladder. Lying on the ground several feet from the back of the mausoleum, it seemed way out of place.

There weren't trees, power lines, or anything that someone might have used a ladder for. Except possibly getting to the roof?

TJ leaned the ladder against the back wall and began to climb. Parker's scent grew stronger as the wind carried it toward him. Gazing over the edge, TJ saw Parker stretched out on the pebbles of the flat roof. He got to him with a quick leap from the rungs of the ladder.

The fighting inside had continued without either Byron or Charles making much of an impact on the other. Even with one arm incapacitated, Charles was able to hold off Byron's attacks.

Then they both heard the movement from above that told them someone was moving on the roof. Charles was distracted for a split second thinking that Parker was not only still alive, but had somehow gotten free. Byron saw his chance to make a move.

He grabbed the wrist connected to Charles's shattered elbow and pulled. The pain was enough that Charles couldn't pull back to stop his forward motion. Before Charles could counter this attack, Byron was at his back and had one arm firmly around his neck with his other hand grasping his chin. From this position, Byron could snap Charles neck with little effort.

Charles only had one usable arm, so his single defense was to grasp the inside of Byron's wrist to keep that arm from twisting his head and delivering the killing maneuver. They were frozen in that position, both trying to exert enough strength to overpower the other. Eventually, one of them would weaken.

TJ appeared in the doorway as they struggled.

"Parker's near death on the roof," he gasped.

Byron tried again to deliver the killing twist to Charles's neck, but couldn't accomplish it with Charles's strength pushing his hand in the opposite direction. If he couldn't kill him, he had to incapacitate him until they could help Parker.

Byron bent his knee and swung his foot to the front of Charles leg. Then, with as much force as he could muster from that awkward position, Byron slammed his heal into the front of Charles's knee, snapping it instantly. Charles started to fall and Byron let go to watch him crumple to the floor.

As much as Byron wanted to see Charles dead, he wanted to get to Parker more. Besides, The Assembly needed to question Charles. He slammed his fist into Charles's jaw, knocking him out. Byron and TJ dashed around the building and up the ladder, leaving Charles spread out on the floor.

Parker's face and hands, exposed to the sun, were red, swollen and blistered. The chains holding him to the roof cut into his skin, and dried blood pooled around his waist and trailed from his mouth, nose and several gashes across his face.

Byron couldn't believe he was still alive, but his heart was beating faintly. "Another hour of daylight and ..." Byron started, but couldn't finish.

"He's getting away!" TJ gasped and pointed toward the grass behind the mausoleum. Charles was limping heavily, but still running faster than any human could toward the adjacent woods.

"Forget him," Byron whispered. "We have to take care of Parker."

They both started pulling the bolts holding the chains out of the roof. Once they had him free, Byron picked him up and carried him to the edge of the roof. Ignoring the ladder, he jumped to the ground with Parker in his arms and ran toward the edge of the cemetery.

TJ had his phone out and was calling Quinton before he too jumped from the roof. Quinton would get everyone else back to their meeting place. Within minutes they'd all gathered around Byron and Parker.

* * *

We got the message that Byron had Parker, and my heart leapt. Then I saw him. My God, he looked horrible, destroyed. It was hard to believe that he was still alive after what Charles and a full day of sun had done to him. I stared at him in shock as Byron laid him gently on the grass.

I wanted to run to him and throw my arms around him, never letting him go. But I was afraid I'd hurt him more. He seemed so helpless.

"We have to find someone to feed him," Byron said looking toward TJ and Quinton.

Quinton nodded and turned to leave, but Chris touched his shoulder. "I'll feed him," Chris said quietly to Byron. Our mouths all fell open.

"Are you sure?" Byron asked.

"I think. What do I have to do?"

"He won't be strong enough to feed himself. I'll bite your wrist, and we'll let the blood drip into his mouth."

"I can do that," Chris answered with a subtle nod.

"He may gain consciousness and not want to stop. We'll pull you away from him if necessary."

Chris looked a little less confident. "Okay," he said.

"Luke, Holly, you should leave while we do this," Byron said. "We'll meet you at the cars."

"But Byron ..." I started.

"Come on, Holly," Luke said taking my arm, "let's not take any chances with Chris."

I looked from Luke to Chris, realized what could happen, and agreed. I hadn't fed for a couple days and I sure wouldn't want a repeat performance of what I'd done to Parker. Luke and I took off for the cars.

They showed up about ten minutes later with Byron still carrying the unconscious Parker. This was bad. Both Luke and Quinton had been badly injured but had come out of it as soon as they smelled a human close enough to feed.

"Did you do it?" I asked Chris as Byron put Parker in the back of the SUV and climbed in with him.

Parker didn't look any better. He still looked like he might be dead.

"Twice." Chris was frowning and they all looked worried. "We know we got some blood in him, but it didn't faze him. Byron's really upset about it."

I climbed in the back seat and knelt facing the back to talk to Byron and keep my eye on Parker. "Is he going to be okay?" I asked as Quinton started to drive us away.

"It's bad, Holly," Byron said as he stared down at Parker's face. "We should see some healing soon, but we'll have to feed him again right away when we get back to Rule the Night."

"But he's going to be alright, isn't he?" I needed Byron's reassurance. Looking at Parker, I didn't see how anyone could heal themselves from such horrible injuries, but if Byron said Parker would get better, I could believe it.

Byron took my hand that was hanging over the back seat and looked from Parker to me. "Sweetheart, I don't know. It was cloudy today, so he didn't get as much sun as he might have, but it depends on how much strength he has left. I just don't know."

Well, that's not what I needed to hear, and the look on Byron's face said more than his words ever could. He looked almost haunted. Haunted by his fear that Parker wouldn't survive.

He gave my hand a little squeeze and we both looked back down at Parker's face. His poor face that had been beaten by Charles and ravaged by the sun.

His soft, full lips were cracked, swollen and covered with dried blood. Hell, most of his face was covered with dried blood. His nose was horribly broken and his eyes were so swollen, I didn't know if he'd be able to open them if he was awake.

Overall, though, the most horrific injury was the red, blistered damage from the sun. It was so hard to look at and imagine the pain that came with it. Chained on that roof, Parker couldn't do anything except endure the pain and debilitating rays beating down on him all day.

I hated looking at him, but couldn't turn my eyes away. Somewhere under all that mutilation, I could still see Parker. If he could survive what Charles had done to him, then I could endure seeing that damage.

Maybe he somehow knew that we were there, that we had him now. Maybe he could feel the love I was feeling and trying to send him. I'd always heard that unconscious humans were sometimes aware of people around them. Maybe Parker was aware of us.

"Parker," I whispered, "we're taking care of you and you'll be better soon. Stay strong and don't worry. I love you. I won't let you leave me."

Byron looked up at me and tried to smile. He'd had his hand on Parker's chest right over his heart since he'd sat next to him in the back of the SUV. His other hand was still holding mine. The three of us were connected and we wouldn't let him die.

The two hour drive back to Adelle seemed to take forever, but Byron and I never let go of each other or Parker. Crystal met us at the employee entrance as we pulled up. Byron got out, but left Parker lying there.

"Chris, I hate to ask it of you, but I'd like to feed him again before we move him," Byron said.

"No problem," Chris answered. "I feel fine."

"You couldn't have lost more than about half a pint in the other feedings." Then he hesitated. "Lorna, how much have you taken from him?"

"Very little," she answered. "Only a few ounces."

"Good," Byron said.

As bad as Parker was, Byron was still concerned about Chris's health. Chris was my brother and I hadn't thought about him losing too much blood. I should have.

Byron and Chris climbed in the back of the SUV while Luke, Crystal and I went on inside. We went down to Parker's suite and Crystal turned down his bed while I found a pair of the flannel pajama bottoms he liked to sleep in. Luke went into the bathroom and filled a small tub with warm water to wash the blood off him.

Byron carried Parker in, laid him gently on the bed, and began to remove his dirty, blood-stained clothes. We'd seen the injuries to Parker's face, but the bruises on his chest and back where Charles had obviously kicked him were disgusting. Worse, still, was the long gash across his abdomen.

"Taping it might make it easier to heal," TJ said.

Byron nodded without saying anything. From the look on his face I got the idea that he was on the edge of losing it. Staying quiet helped him keep control.

TJ got some of that white medical tape from the bathroom. Byron pressed the edges of the slash together as TJ placed several pieces of tape across it. Then Byron started to wash off all the blood.

We usually healed fast enough that bandages were just a waste of time. When Luke and Quinton had been injured, they'd both been fed and their wounds were left to heal on their own. Parker was just too weak to heal that quickly.

The sun does that to us and Charles made sure Parker had a full-day's dose of those rays beating down on him. Obviously, Charles had thought Parker would die before Byron got to him, and I honestly didn't know why he was still alive. Maybe there had been more clouds than I realized. Maybe the huge, old trees in the cemetery had shaded him as the sun moved across the sky. Whatever the reason, I knew that he could have easily died from Charles's torture.

With my thoughts, the tears were quietly rolling down my cheeks again as I watched Byron take care of Parker. It seemed like Byron needed to do everything for Parker himself, which I understood. I wanted to do everything for him, too.

I felt Chris slide his arm around my shoulder and lean gently against me. There wasn't much for any of us to say, so being close helped deal with all the emotions swirling around.

"Thanks for feeding him," I whispered. It kinda' seemed lame to just say thanks like that when voluntarily feeding a vampire was way out there.

"He swallowed and licked his lip a little that last time," Chris whispered back.

"Really?"

"Yeah, but didn't open his eyes or anything."

"What did Byron say?"

"Nothing. But he looked like he was glad to see it."

They got Parker cleaned up and in the pajama bottoms, then pulled the covers up over him. Nothing to do now except wait for his natural healing ability to take care of him.

TJ and Quinton headed for the guard office, and Luke followed Crystal down to the bar.

"Chris," Lorna said, "you look exhausted."

"It's been a long night," he shrugged.

For the first time, I noticed that Chris was covered with dried blood from shooting the vampires in the bar. Besides his clothes, there were spots and drips on his face and arms, even in his hair. After all that, he'd fed Parker three times. We couldn't have done all this without him. I stared at his face, not finding any words to thank him enough.

"And a long day, and a long night before that," Lorna said. "I'm putting you to bed before I relieve the front door guard. You need some sleep."

"You got a deal," Chris smiled as he slid his arm around her waist. Then smiled and whispered. "Promise to wake me at dawn?"

I knew he meant for only Lorna to hear that last part, but he forgot how much vampires can hear. They left with their arms around each other, and I couldn't resist a little smile.

"They care a lot for each other," Byron said.

"Yeah. It's nice seeing Chris happy."

I took the tub full of now cold, bloody water that they'd used to clean Parker into the bathroom. I dumped it, refilled it with hot, soapy water, and grabbed a clean wash cloth to take them back out to Byron.

"You've still got blood on your face," I said as I rang out the cloth and started to wipe his face. His wounds were now all healed, though.

"You too," Byron said glancing up at me. "I could go to the sink," he sighed, but I knew he was just so tired and worried that he probably wouldn't have.

"You're taking care of Parker, so I'll take care of you," I answered. "I'll shower when I leave."

"Thank you." I saw a tiny smile on his lips, but his eyes were still so sad.

It would be a while before we got to see his usual cheerful smile back on his face. Not until Parker was better. Even then, the thought of what Parker'd gone through would haunt him and all of us for a really long time.

"It looks like the cut on your cheekbone was a bad one, but it's almost healed."

"Charles got in some good hits, but I'm okay."

"How bad was Charles when he left?"

"Broken elbow, broken knee, and bloodier than me. I wish I'd killed him immediately when I had the chance."

"The most important thing is that you got Parker back and he'll be fine, now."

"Sweetheart ..." Byron hesitated before he said anything else. When he called me sweetheart, he was going to say something I didn't want to hear. "You need to understand that Parker may not be okay."

"What do you mean?" I sat down on the bed next to Byron. "He still might die?"

"No, I'm sure he'll heal. But he may not be able to control the bloodthirst."

"Why not? You'll teach him and we'll all help."

"Because of the way Charles changed him. TJ told you that he used the old methods."

"I don't understand ..."

"You remember that it took days for you to change because I fed you slowly. When you tasted your first human blood, you couldn't stop on your own, so we stopped you. Then we watched you and encouraged you to find the control you needed.

"Centuries ago, we were all changed in one night like Parker was, then we were left to feed on our own. We killed, and no one tried to stop us or tell us we shouldn't. Once the Assembly formed and imposed the new rule against killing, most of us had a difficult time controlling our instincts, but eventually learned. Those who couldn't learn control, or didn't want to, were executed."

"I'm sure Parker will. He won't want to kill anyone." My voice was determined, but also full of fear.

"The ones that had the hardest time were the young ones. No one under a few years old could get the control they needed. Parker is only a few days old, and Charles let him feed and kill at least three times. I don't see how he'll be able to control the bloodthirst now. I tried to help many young ones, but none of them succeeded."

"What happened to them?"

"The Assembly had to execute them." His voice was so soft and so sad when he said that.

"No!" I jumped to my feet and folded my arms across my waist like a stubborn child, holding myself. "The Assembly couldn't do that. I won't let them!"

"We may not have a choice," Byron said quietly, sorrowfully.

Now I was mad. The kind of mad when you can't stop crying, so you start yelling. "So you're just going to give up and turn him over to them? That's not going to happen. We'll run away, and I'll take care of him."

"So you can watch him kill every night? Or do you think you'll be strong enough to pull him off? You won't be. You'll be hunted down, and I won't be able to stop it."

"At least I won't be giving up on him," my voice broke as my tears continued. At least we weren't yelling anymore. "You sound like you've already given up."

"I haven't given up. I'm going to do everything I can," Byron put his arms around my shoulders. I didn't hug him back, though, because my arms were still wrapped around my own waist.

"Holly, I just need you to understand that it might not work," he said quietly.

"I understand, but I won't accept it. We'll have to find some way to make it work."

We both heard Parker move. His head rolled to the side and he moved his arm from the bed to cross his chest, but he didn't open his eyes. I sat on the bed next to him and took his hand. Byron went over to the other side of the bed.

"Parker," I said quietly.

"Don't fight," he answered with his eyes still closed.

"I'm sorry we woke you," Byron said.

"I'm hungry," Parker said as he finally opened his eyes and looked at Byron.

"I'll call TJ to bring you someone."

Byron stood and took his phone from his pocket to call TJ. He stepped away from the bed and talked quietly. Parker never took his eyes off Byron.

"Parker," I said quietly while I gently squeezed his hand. It took several seconds, but he finally turned his head to look at me. "I was so worried about you."

The look on his face puzzled me. It was like he didn't know what I was talking about.

"I'm okay. Will you feed me?" he asked.

Then I understood. He was so distracted, so consumed, by his hunger that he couldn't think of anything else, not even me.

"Byron's taking care of that," I whispered. Parker nodded and turned to watch Byron again.

When my hunger was at its worst during my change, when it seemed to be all I was, I still thought of Parker. I still longed for him and forced myself to gain control so I could see him.

How bad must his hunger be if it made him ignore me? Or did he not love me enough to fight his instinct to feed? That thought scared me. Nothing was more important to me than my love for Parker.

The way Charles changed Parker created bloodthirst. I knew that was so much worse than the hunger I felt during my change. But Parker wasn't in the midst of change, he was waking from a horrible injury.

I didn't know what to think, but I knew how I felt. I felt like Parker didn't love me anymore. What would I do if that was true? Did he care more about feeding than he cared for me?

Without warning, a hiccupping sob escaped from my lips. I'd been gently weeping, but couldn't control it anymore.

The sound caught Parker's attention. He glanced over to me, looked confused again, and looked back at Byron who was heading back toward the bed. The expression on his face for Byron was one of anticipation, almost longing. It was the look I wanted him to have when he looked at me.

I let go of his hand and quietly walked toward the bedroom door. I passed through the living room of his suite feeling numb and met TJ at the door to the hallway. He had his arm around a woman's shoulders. I didn't look at either of them.

Quinton and Lorna followed TJ. If Byron had asked for all three of them to help feed Parker, he must have thought Parker would put up quite a fight. It had taken all of them to get me off Parker when I attacked him. Even weakened from the sun and horribly injured, Parker would fight them. It would be bad.

"I'll wait in the common area," I said as I passed them.

Chapter 12

Parker smelled the nearness of a human before they brought her into his bedroom. The scent of her blood, the sound of her beating heart, and the imagined sound of her cries as she struggled in his arms made him long to leap from the bed and taste her.

But the weakness from his forced exposure to the sun kept him flat on his back. All he could do was raise his head an inch off the pillow and turn his body slightly toward the door.

Her blood, though, would strengthen him. Once she was empty, he would be full. Her blood would give him the power to finish healing.

Why were they taking so long? Didn't they know how much he needed her blood? Couldn't they understand how much he ached to feed? His fangs were fully extended, his lips were drawn back, and his eyes glared at the door with anticipation.

"Parker!" Byron said forcefully, trying to get his attention.

Parker heard Byron, glanced at his face, but turned his eyes back to the door. He knew she was right on the other side.

"They won't bring her in until you listen to me." Byron moved to block Parker's view of the door and try to get him to listen.

"What?" Parker asked. His irritation was clear in his voice.

"We won't allow you to drain her."

Parker found he could move his head enough to look around Byron, so he stared again at the door and didn't even bother to answer.

Byron took Parker's face in his hands and turned his head so he couldn't see the door anymore. Parker could only see Byron and was getting angry with the interference in his desire to feed. He didn't bother trying to keep that anger off his face.

"You have to listen to her blood and stop when the flow changes. Do you understand? You have to stop feeding before you've taken enough to harm her."

"Let me feed!"

Byron could hear the need in Parker's voice and knew he was asking Parker to do something he probably wouldn't be able to accomplish. Parker may never be able to control the bloodthirst, but they had to try. If they couldn't train him to feed with control, he would have to be executed, and Bryon couldn't allow himself to consider that possibility.

"Do you understand?" Byron asked again.

"Yes!" Parker spat out the answer that he knew Byron wanted to hear. The truth, though, was that Parker didn't even remember what Byron was asking of him.

"Tell me," Byron said forcefully. "Tell me you will try to stop feeding before you harm her."

Parker looked confused. He understood the words but couldn't really grasp the concept of what Byron said. Somehow, though, he knew Byron wouldn't let him feed until he agreed.

"I'll try to stop," he said automatically, just repeating the words.

Byron let go of Parker and headed for the door. Parker didn't get it. His response that he would try was only spoken to get Byron to let him feed, but they had to start somewhere. Turning Parker from bloodthirst would be a long and difficult process if it was possible at all.

TJ, Lorna and Quinton walked the woman into the bedroom, and Byron watched Parker strain toward them. His eyes were wide as he stared at her neck, and his fingers clenched as if he was trying to grasp her.

"You'll take her wrist," Byron said with as much authority as he could, but he wasn't sure Parker even heard him.

TJ sat her on the bed and Parker's hand moved with as much strength as he could muster to clench over her knee. It was the only part of her he could reach.

Byron lifted her wrist and bit into it. Parker growled with rage thinking that Byron was going to steal his prey. He strained again to move toward them, but could barely lift his head or twist his shoulders.

Parker wanted to tear her away from Byron. He wanted to claim the blood he so desperately needed, but he was helpless.

Parker was surprised when Byron didn't drink her blood, but moved the wrist toward Parker's mouth. Once he could smell the drops of blood that oozed from the puncture marks in her wrist only inches from his face, he forgot that anyone else was in the room. Now his only thought was of his need and the blood that he was about to taste.

Parker sucked deeply on her wrist as soon as it touched his lips. The taste filling his mouth almost overwhelmed him. It was ecstasy, and he could feel his strength growing as the salty, metallic liquid slid down his throat.

With immediate, renewed strength, he was able to reach up with both hands and press that wrist against his mouth as he drew harder on her vein. Somewhere in his head, he knew the other three vampires were watching him. Were they thinking of taking her for themselves?

Feeling the renewal her blood was giving him, he rolled away from them onto his side stretching the woman's arm to keep it at his lips. He pulled his knees up to his chest attempting to cradle her arm to him to claim this prize that he wasn't willing to share.

"You need to stop now, Parker," Byron said.

Parker heard the voice saying something to him but refused to acknowledge it. He had the only thing he wanted, the thing he so desperately needed, and nothing else mattered. In his mind, nothing else of any importance even existed.

He felt hands on him, turning him onto his back. That voice kept telling him to stop feeding. Someone pried his hands away from the woman's wrists while other fingers were forcing his jaws apart. Some small voice in the background kept trying to tell him to stop, but how could he pay any attention to it when they were stealing his prey?

Struggling with all his growing strength, he tried to fight them off, but they were too much for his battered body. Her blood stopped flowing down his throat and her wrist was no longer pressed to his mouth.

Parker screamed out his rage as he thrashed about the bed trying to win his prey back from them. He punched, kicked and twisted frantically to escape from the hands holding him down, but they were just too strong. He was helpless to do anything except scream unintelligible curses at them and bang his head against the pillow.

But he couldn't just let them steal her away from him. He continued to fight even after the smell of her blood and the beat of her heart faded and he knew she'd been taken out of the room.

Holly sat alone on a couch in the common area. Through two closed doors and down a long hallway, she could faintly hear Parker's frenzied cries. It sounded so much like a predatory animal battling for its life that it was hard to believe her sweet, loving Parker was making those sounds.

But she knew it was him, and she knew what caused him to scream out like that. They'd had to pry the woman away from him, and he was enraged. His beast was fighting for its prey. She must have sounded the same as they dragged her off Parker.

Quinton walked toward her with the woman who was still unaware of where she was or what had just happened to her. He gazed at Holly for a moment as he passed with a mixture of sorrow, sympathy, and concern. He looked like he was trying to make himself smile some reassurance for her, but didn't succeed at all.

They didn't say anything to each other because there was nothing to say. They both knew how the feeding had gone. From Parker's continued screams and curses, they both knew he was still fighting to get his prey back.

By the time the commotion in Parker's room settled down, Quinton was coming back down the stairs without the woman. His fangs were still visible, huge and making it hard for him to comfortably keep his lips closed. Holly knew Byron, TJ and Lorna would be the same after watching Parker feed and not yet feeding themselves.

"I'll come with you," Holly said quietly as she got up from the couch and walked toward Quinton.

"Maybe you should wait for Byron," Quinton answered.

"You're all desperate to feed. I can stay with Parker while you find donors."

"Maybe you're right," he sighed.

Holly could hear his hunger in his voice, so she put her arm through his to offer some comfort. Besides, she needed the comfort and reassurance as much, if not more, than he did.

Parker sat up leaning against the headboard, staring toward his feet while everyone else stood around the room. He was still angry, but was able to restrain his violent emotions. Holly could feel the hunger from the others like she could from Quinton.

"I'll stay with him while the four of you feed," she said quietly to Byron. He looked distracted from his hunger, and didn't answer her. She thought he still may not be willing to leave.

"You need to feed," she repeated.

Byron looked at TJ, Lorna, and Quinton, and nodded his head toward the door. They left without hesitation. The bar was still open, so it wouldn't take them long to find the donors they needed.

"I don't think he's strong enough to get out of bed, or at least not go very far if he does," Byron said as soon as they'd left. "Call immediately if there are any problems."

"We'll be fine," I said quietly, touching his arm.

Byron glanced over at Parker for a second. He was still staring and declaring his anger with the expression on his face. He never looked at Byron.

When Byron was gone, Holly went over to sit on the bed next to Parker and she took his hand. He turned his head toward her and the anger dissipated from his face. He gazed at her as if he was seeing her for the first time and couldn't get enough of her face.

"Holly," he sighed and reached his other hand up to cup her cheek like he was making sure she was real.

"How are you, Parker?"

Without answering, Parker moved his hand from her cheek to the back of her head and slowly pulled her toward him. He continued to gaze into her eyes when their faces were merely inches apart, then leaned in and kissed her.

Parker pulled his hand out of hers and wrapped his arm around her waist. They moved to hold each other firmly, yet gently, while never releasing their lips. He leaned back against the pillows pulling Holly with him, and held her tighter against his chest.

She wasn't ready to break their kiss, but his lips left hers as he moved to kiss her jaw and then her neck.

"I missed you so much," he whispered. She felt the warmth of his kiss and the vibration of his voice right below her ear. "I never thought I'd see you again."

He continued nuzzling her neck. "I thought..." Holly's voice broke into quiet tears as she spoke. "I thought Charles would kill you."

"Oh, babe," he answered. He moved his lips away from her neck and buried his face in her hair while he swayed back and forth as if he was gently rocking her. "I love you so much. I hate that you were so worried."

Holly could hardly believe that she was in Parker's arms again feeling his strength and warmth and hearing him say that he loved her. But she couldn't let this go any further. She needed to think. She moved away from him enough to look in his eyes, but still didn't let go of their embrace.

"I know that feeding was hard, but Byron will keep helping you and you'll be fine."

The anger started to show on Parker's face again and he let go of Holly. "Byron didn't help me," he said as if he was accusing Byron of something. "I needed to feed more and they took her away. They stole her from me!"

"They didn't steal her. You know we have to control our instincts when we feed, so we don't harm humans. They kept you from hurting her."

"But they hurt *me*. I need blood to finish healing, and they kept me from getting enough. Once I'm healed and have my full strength back, there'll be plenty of time to work on control."

"You would have drained her."

"That's only because I'm a new vampire. Charles said all new vampires drain their donors. That's how we get strong."

"He lied to you, Parker. I've never drained a human."

"You'd be stronger if you had."

"That's not true. That's the kind of stuff Armand tried to tell me, but it was all lies."

"He said Byron didn't want to tell me the whole truth while I was still human."

"He made you bloodthirsty on purpose. Then he beat you, slashed your stomach, and chained you on the roof to die in the sunshine. He knew that if you somehow survived, you'd still be bloodthirsty, and the Assembly would have to execute you."

"Why would he do that?" The look on Parker's face surprised me, as if he really didn't know what Charles's evil mind was capable of.

"To get back at Byron for destroying all his plans. If you can't control the bloodthirst, Byron will either have to let you kill or turn you over to the Assembly for execution. Byron will have to turn against everything he believes in. Or he'll have to watch you die."

"I was glad that Charles changed me," Parker practically whispered. "I was afraid that Byron never would."

"He would have done it. But he'd have done it right so you'd be able to control your instincts and not hurt anyone."

"I'll learn to control it," Parker said with determination.

"It won't be easy. It's the way Charles changed you, and we can't do anything about that. You'll have to really try to do everything Byron tells you."

"I will. Would you help me up, Holly? I'm tired of sitting in this bed."

Parker said the words that I wanted to hear, but I knew that he didn't really mean it. He was changing the subject so I would stop talking about control, but I'd let him get away with it for now. There'd be plenty of chance to talk about it later.

* * *

Constance stared at the unfamiliar number on her cell and debated whether or not to let it go to voicemail. They'd worked through the night and into the daylight hours on trying to find Charles after Byron destroyed his club in Columbus, and she was tired.

At the last minute, she decided to answer. What difference did it make if she listened to the caller's problem now or in a few minutes when she'd access the message? Maybe it would be easier to just deal with the issue and get it over with.

"So, Constance," said the arrogant voice that she recognized immediately. "When will you be apprehending Byron's son?"

"I have no idea what you're talking about, Charles. Stop playing games, and get to the point."

"Are you saying that Byron hasn't yet reported that his son is bloodthirsty?" Charles's voice was filled with false surprise. "Maybe he simply took care of the execution himself."

"What have you done?" She didn't really need to ask. There was only one way a human became bloodthirsty within a few days.

Charles laughed, but his voice was cold. "Believe me, Constance, he *is* bloodthirsty. If Byron hasn't reported this to you, then he's hiding his son. The punishment for hiding a bloodthirsty vampire is death, if I'm not mistaken."

"Charles!" Constance shouted into the phone even though she knew he'd ended the call. "You sick bastard," she said quietly staring at the phone in her hand.

* * *

By the time I'd left Parker's suite it was 3:30 in the morning. I was dead tired, knew that I wouldn't be able to fall asleep for a while, but couldn't stand the thought of sitting alone in my room. What I needed more than anything was the peace and quiet I got from the darkness out on the streets. I needed to think, and Parker's kiss gave me some serious stuff to think about.

Quinton and TJ were checking the remote cameras in the guard office when I got to the employee door.

"I'm going for a walk," I told them.

"Sorry, Holly," TJ answered, "but no one's supposed to be out alone. Byron thinks Charles may send someone to Adelle."

"Oh," I said. I'm sure they saw the disappointment on my face.

"Don't you usually walk with Byron?" Quinton asked.

"He's with Parker," I answered.

"I'll go with you if you'd like," Quinton said. "If you can spare me here, TJ?"

TJ gave him a funny look, but I didn't know what that was about.

"No problem," TJ said, still looking at Quinton. "We're about done, and Lorna's got the perimeter."

"Thanks, Quinton," I said.

We walked without talking for about half a block. "How was Parker?" Quinton asked breaking our silence.

"Good. He was alert and talking. I helped him out of bed so he could sit somewhere else. When I left, he asked Byron to help him shower."

"That's good. He's getting his strength back."

We walked in silence again. Thin clouds were scooting across the almost full moon and a warm spring breeze blew gently through the trees. The dogwoods were blooming and one of the petals was loosened by the wind and floated down to us. Quinton caught it. I smiled and he handed it to me.

"How, um ... are you and Parker? I mean, are the two of you good?"

"Yeah," I smiled more. "I think so."

"That's good."

"Quinton, can I ask you something?"

"Sure, Holly. Anything you want."

I had so much on my mind, so many questions, but one thing kept eating away at me. "Parker and I kissed, but it was different. I ... Oh, never mind." I felt my eyes fill with tears right before one ran down my cheek.

Quinton put his hand on my shoulder and stopped walking. "What is it, Holly? You can ask me."

"Well ..." I was still hesitating, not sure if I wanted to share my thoughts, but I needed answers. "Before, the scent of his blood and the taste of his lips made me crazy. I wanted him so much, I had to stay completely away from him. Tonight, it was ... it was different."

"He was human then, and your instincts wanted you to feed. That part's gone now, is all."

"But what if desire for his blood was all I ever felt? What if I never really loved him, but only wanted him to feed me?" There.

I'd said it. My worst fear was blurted out into the night. That didn't slow down my tears any.

"I don't know. I haven't been involved with a human since I became a vampire. Weren't you in love with Parker before your change?"

"I thought so, but I might have just been attracted to a hot guy." I shook my head at my own lameness. "I don't know how I feel, and that scares me. I don't want to hurt him."

"Are you saying you don't love him anymore?"

"No! I think I love him, but ... I'm not as sure as I used to be."

"Give yourself time. He's changed, and you need to get used to the new Parker. And we still don't know how he'll respond to training."

"So it might not matter if I love him or not because the Assembly might have to execute him anyway, is that it?" I blurted out. "How could you say that?" I was suddenly mad as hell.

"That's not what I meant. I'm sorry, Holly. I just meant give him time. Trying to get control is going to be really hard."

"I didn't mean to yell at you," I said shaking my head and looking away from him. "It's just that ... Damn it!" My voice grew softer and I looked back into his eyes as I made myself face the truth. "You're right. We may lose him anyway."

"Byron will do everything he can. He won't give up on Parker."

"No, he won't." I looked back, right into Quinton's eyes. "And neither will I."

We headed back toward Rule the Night and I slipped my arm in his like I always did with Byron. I wasn't talking because I was thinking about Parker. I didn't know what Quinton was thinking about.

Dawn was ready to break over the horizon when TJ opened the employee door for us.

"I'm going to check on Parker," I said to both of them. "Thanks, Quinton," I added as I got on my tiptoes to give him a peck on the cheek.

He gave me a funny look. "Anytime," he mumbled.

* * *

"That was interesting," TJ said as he squinted at Quinton.

"No big deal. I helped her figure out some stuff."

"Figure out some stuff? What?"

Quinton looked like he didn't really want to answer. "Not that it's any of your business, but Holly said she's not sure she loves Parker anymore."

"And you took that as the opening you've been waiting for." The words were clearly not a question, but an accusation.

"Oh, yeah! An eighteen-year-old girls tells me she's upset and confused, so I take that as the chance to make a move on her. Is that the kind of guy you think I am?" Quinton looked like he wanted to punch TJ.

"I know how you feel about her," TJ answered, facing the anger in Quinton's face.

"And I thought you knew that I have no intentions of doing anything about it."

"Then what was that kiss for?"

"Shit, man," Quinton sighed. "A little nothing on my cheek, right in front of you. What do you think it was? She said thank you because I convinced her to give Parker time."

"You did?"

"Of course I did." Their anger had diminished, but their stares showed the tension was still there.

"Sorry, man," TJ finally said quietly while shaking his head. "It just seemed that you jumped at the chance to go for a walk and be alone with her."

"Yeah, I jumped at the chance," Quinton nodded. "But that's all. Besides, I know she loves Parker. Even when we were at Nibble and pretending to be involved, she talked about *him* whenever we were alone."

"I figured you spent all your time protecting her from Charles and Armand."

Quinton grinned. "Ya' know, she wasn't really afraid of Charles and Armand. Her biggest fear was that Parker would hate her because she attacked him."

"Parker spent all his time figuring out how he was going to get away from Byron so he could see Holly."

"It doesn't matter how I feel," Quinton shrugged. "Nothing's going to come between them. I know that."

* * *

I knocked gently on Parker's door because I thought he could be sleeping, but I immediately heard his voice telling me to come in. Before I got the door completely opened, he was there ready to hug me.

"Hi, babe," he whispered into my ear as we hugged and he kissed my cheek.

Parker looked sleepy which wasn't surprising since it must be full daylight outside by now. Byron, however, looked exhausted. I wondered when he'd last slept.

"Are you going to get some sleep today?" I asked as I walked toward the couch to sit next to Byron.

He smiled. "TJ will be here in about ten minutes, and I'll be on my way to bed."

"TJ hasn't had much rest, either. I'll stay with Parker."

"That's not really a good idea," he said looking concerned. Then he glanced over at Parker. Parker's face was worried, too.

"Why not?" I asked both of them. Parker looked at Byron and nodded slightly like it was okay to tell me something.

"Parker's not completely healed yet, and isn't on a regular feeding schedule. He may wake up with an overwhelming desire to feed, and you wouldn't be strong enough to stop him."

I looked over at Parker and I must have had that same worried expression because Parker reached for my hand.

"I don't know how I'm going to react to hunger. I don't want to fight you to try getting out of here."

"So you're afraid of me," I grinned to try lightening the mood a little.

He tugged on the hand he was holding and pulled me back to my feet. His arms circled my waist and he lifted me off the floor. I giggled as he spun me around with my feet flying out a little behind me and my arms grasped firmly around his neck.

We stopped face and face, and he said, "I'll get better and learn to control this as soon as possible. For you."

"I know you will."

"Here's my replacement," Byron said as we all became aware of TJ's scent right before he knocked on the door.

I gave Parker a quick kiss, he and TJ went toward the bedroom, and Byron and I left. As tired as Parker looked, I knew he'd sleep soundly. He'd also sleep without worry because he knew TJ would be glaring at him from the chair, ready to stop him from going out to feed.

Byron and I walked slowly down the hall to my room, then he'd continue to his suite. The whole atmosphere of Rule the Night was different since Charles took Parker. We all felt the apprehension of not knowing how this horrible episode would end and it hung over our lives like a dark cloud.

"How is Crystal?" I asked. She'd taken over the responsibility of keeping Rule the Night running normally. At least normal as far as the clients and the human customers were concerned.

"I've barely seen her since we said goodbye when we left for Columbus. I know she's running this place as well as I ever have." I could hear the respect in Byron's voice. He was proud of the woman he loved.

"She's doing it for you, you know."

"I know," he nodded.

"I think I should get back to work tonight. With Crystal spending a lot of time in the office, Luke's alone at the bar."

"Chris helped him earlier," Byron smiled. "He doesn't know much about bartending, but I heard the two of them kept the customers entertained and happy."

"I'll bet they did," I smiled back.

"Goodnight, Holly," he said as we stopped at my door. "I know you're worried about Parker, but try to get some sleep."

"I wish I could help him more."

"I know. So do I."

Chapter 13

Three days went past with very little change. Parker wasn't allowed to wander on his own, so he spent his time in his suite with different ones of us visiting, and watching him, at different times.

I worked the bar most of the hours we were open and Parker slept every day with one of the oldest, strongest vampires guarding him. We didn't see each other much and only had a few minutes at a time to be alone. Parker was right there down the hall from me, yet I still missed him.

No one talked much about his feeding. It took longer to recover from exposure to the sun than it did to heal from normal injuries, and he needed blood to help him, so Byron was feeding him every night.

I was kept away while that was going on, but Byron kept me informed. He told me there wasn't any improvement. He also said, though, that the process of breaking bloodthirst took time and progress was slow, so I told him I wasn't too worried.

That was a lie. I was worried, and troubled, not to mention overwhelmingly sad. I wanted Parker to be okay, and I wanted him to find the control he needed. I wanted all that right away. It was so hard to be patient and not know how things were going to turn out. I was sure we all felt the same and simply carried on as if we were fine.

Luke, Chris and I closed the bar one night as usual, and I was looking forward to spending my time until dawn with Parker. Byron wouldn't let Chris do any valet parking as long as there was the possibility that Charles could be around, but that didn't matter to me because I loved working with Chris. Not being able to see Parker very often, being with Chris every night somehow comforted me.

I left the bar while the two of them finished cleaning up and I headed right to my room to clean myself up a little before visiting Parker. As I came out of my room to go to his suite, I heard someone running hard down the steps.

I looked down the hall to see Parker racing toward me, but I don't think he saw me at all. He threw himself into his suite moving as fast as only a vampire can. I ran to him.

Parker stood in the middle of his living room with his hands covering his face. He was trembling so violently, I thought he might fall over any second. I had no idea what could have happened or what he'd been doing upstairs.

"Parker?" I said quietly. My tone of voice asked what was wrong.

His hands came down, his eyes flew open, and before I could blink he was throwing his body against mine.

"Hold me!" he gasped.

I held him and every muscle in his body shook as he cried into my hair. I couldn't imagine what on earth had upset him so much. For that matter, why was he alone?

After several minutes his shaking slowed and his sobs quieted. "What happened?" I finally asked and started to pull away to look in his face.

"Don't let go," he practically begged.

I squeezed him tighter with my arms around his back and waited for him to start talking.

"Byron said he thought I could be alone for a couple hours. I didn't think I was hungry ... wanted to show him that I was doing better and went up to surprise him in his office." His voice was unsteady and almost broke back into sobs as he talked.

"Did the scent of the humans tempt you?"

"Only one," he said hesitantly. "Chris came out of the bar and headed toward me."

"Chris?" I gasped. Did he hurt Chris? Oh, no! Not Chris.

"I ran. I didn't touch him, but … God ... I wanted his blood. If he'd gotten one step closer I couldn't have resisted. I can still smell him, Holly. My fangs ache, they want his blood so bad. Don't let go of me!"

He still had his face buried in my hair. His words were choppy and spoken with obvious strain. I could tell that, even now, he was fighting and straining to find control because his beast wanted to feed from Chris.

"I won't let go." I stroked his back and squeezed even tighter.

He suddenly pulled his head off my shoulder and cried out with a horrible combination of a scream and an animalistic growl. At the same moment, I smelled Sarita right outside his door, only feet away. She was probably just walking down the hallway to her room, but he smelled her, too, and his beast wanted to feed on that human.

It was too much for him. Being so tempted by Chris, the scent of another human shattered any restraint he'd been able to find. But this was Sarita, the only family he had except for Byron. To Parker, Sarita was part sister, part grandmother, and he would normally do anything to protect her and make her happy.

"No, Parker!" I screamed. "Not Sarita!"

He wrenched himself out of my arms and I knew that I had no chance of holding him back. I ran to the door and threw my back against it to keep him from opening it. His fangs were huge and he glared a threat at me while I pulled out my phone to speed dial

Byron. I didn't have time to say a word as Byron answered, but knew he would hear what I was saying to Parker.

"Parker, I won't let you leave."

"Get out of my way!" he bellowed.

"You'll have to go through me," I said with the calmest voice I could find and hoped to calm him also.

"Don't make me hurt you!" I knew from his voice that he didn't want to but would be driven to hurt me if I didn't get away from the door. He sounded so cold, so determined, so unlike Parker.

"Think, Parker," I begged. "You can do it. Push the instincts back. You're not the beast!"

"Yes. I. Am!" he growled, each word getting louder and more intense.

Then he grabbed me by my upper arms, lifted me off the ground, and threw me away from the door. I landed on top of the glass and chrome coffee table, shattering it and a vase that sat on top of it.

I felt several shards of glass pierce through the skin of my shoulder and cheek. What hurt the most, though, was the snap and crunch of my wrist when I landed.

I tried to get up to go back to Parker and do anything I could to stop him from draining Sarita, but another piece of glass went through my thigh as soon as I moved. As I struggled, a hideous cry from Parker scared me to death. Had he gotten to Sarita?

I rolled my shoulders to try getting up again and saw Byron, TJ, and Quinton forcing Parker back through the door. Byron had him around the waist with his shoulder pressed against Parker's chest, and TJ and Quinton each had one arm. Still Parker was hard for them to handle. Bloodthirst gave us insane strength.

Once they were in the room, Lorna came through, went behind Parker, and grabbed his feet off the floor. They carried him into the bedroom face down still struggling with all his might.

While Parker's continued cries and screams assaulted my brain, I sank back down in the middle of all that glass and sobbed. It was the most horrible scene I'd ever experienced, and the look on Parker's face would take me a long time to forget.

Most horrible of all, though, was that he'd been completely controlled by that beast inside him. He knew he was helpless to stop it. He'd admitted that to me and to himself. And he hurt me.

No, Parker hadn't hurt me. His inner beast had done that because I was trying to stop him from getting to his prey. It wasn't the pain from the glass that hurt the most. It was the grief in my heart. If Parker would go after Sarita, he was lost and there was no way to know if we'd ever get him back.

I must have passed out for a few seconds, or minutes, I couldn't tell, because the next thing I knew, I was being lifted out of that bed of glass and metal. A strong arm across my shoulder blades and another under my knees, I was held against a solid chest while someone was quietly saying my name.

"Luke," I sighed, so thankful to see him.

"Let's get you out of here," he tried to smile.

"We'll take care of you," Crystal's voice said from the direction of my feet.

I looked toward her and let out a long breath with a sense of calm coming over me. I guess that sense of calm was really me passing out again because I woke up lying on my left side in my own bed with Crystal wiping my face with a cool cloth.

My shoulder hurt, so I turned my head as far as I could to see what was going on behind me. Luke was there staring at and touching my back.

That's when I realized I was naked except for the sheet draped carefully over me. It was pushed off my back and right arm so Luke could take care of my wounds, but I still felt very exposed.

"That might be it," Luke was saying as he stroked my shoulder. "Nope, here's another."

I felt a pin-prick of pain that disappeared immediately as he pulled out the glass. Then he gently stroked my shoulder again still feeling for more. After a few moments, he taped white medical gauze to my shoulder. I hadn't realized it was bad enough for a bandage.

"My leg," I whispered.

"I'll check," Luke said.

I felt him move lower on the bed as he lifted the sheet off my legs and I realized it then only covered the front of me from chest to hips. I tried to hold it in place and not think about the fact that he had a bird's-eye-view of my bare butt.

"Yeah, here it is." Another pin-prick as he pulled glass out, and then he was stroking my thigh to check for any he might have missed.

"I think we've got it all," Luke said as he pulled the sheet into place to cover me a little more. "Anywhere else, Holly? We don't want you healing with glass inside."

"I think I broke my wrist."

"I was afraid of that, the way it's bruised," Crystal said. "We'll wait for Byron to look at it. He might want to call the doc in to make sure it heals right."

I looked down at my right wrist resting on my hip. It was a horrible color and looked dead. I couldn't move it.

"Let's get you more comfortable," Crystal said. "Roll onto your back, but if you feel any more glass, let us know."

She secured the sheet over me as I rolled, then she straightened it. Each of them grasped me under a shoulder and lifted me higher on the bed so I was half sitting against pillows. Then Crystal pulled a blanket up to join the sheet. I felt much better.

Crystal was looking closely at my cheek. "Is it bad?" I asked.

"The bruise is nasty, but the cut isn't very deep and it's already started healing," she smiled. "You've got dozens of little scratches and cuts all over, but nothing serious."

"Your shoulder was the worst, and you have quite a lump on the side of your head," Luke added, "but they seem to be healing, too."

"How's Parker?" I know my eyes were pleading with them to tell me he was alright.

Luke looked like he didn't know whether to answer me or not, but he did. "He was still fighting them when we left. I'll go check on him and find someone to feed you, okay?"

"Thanks," I whispered.

"Do you feel anymore glass?" Crystal asked once he'd gone.

"No, just achy all over." I was staring at my feet, but then looked up into her eyes. "Parker's really bad, isn't he?"

"I'm afraid so." Her expression was so sorrowful. The same way I looked, I'm sure. "What caused him to lose it like that?" she asked quietly.

Of course none of them knew what had happened. They didn't even know that Parker had gone upstairs. All they knew was what they heard over my phone.

I told her the whole story of how he'd run from Chris but then couldn't resist the scent of human blood when Sarita had walked past his door. By the time I finished we were both crying.

"I could almost understand if they'd been bleeding, but it was just the presence of humans that threw him over the edge," I said as I wiped away a tear that had rolled down to my ear. "Was it that bad for all the old vampires?"

"I think so," she said. "Byron told me that all the old legends about vampires being demons and terrorizing whole villages came from those days. The stories about humans hunting us during the daytime are true, too. They figured out the only way to kill us was to find us sleeping, so they drove stakes through our hearts, burned us, or cut off our heads to make sure we were dead. It must have been a horrible time."

"Until the Assembly realized we didn't have to kill."

"They knew we had to stop killing if we were to live and figured out how to create new vampires and train young ones that could control their instincts. Until then, all new vampires were just left on their own to feed any way they could."

"I didn't think that I could hate Charles any more than I already did, but knowing he made Parker bloodthirsty on purpose ... I really want to kill him."

"We all do."

I caught a whiff of vampire and human approaching my door right before they knocked. Luke, Byron, and Chris. Chris's blood, like any human blood, tempted me a little before I automatically pressed the hunger aside.

We all had to do that when around humans, but we did it so routinely, that we barely noticed it. I silently wished that Parker would someday know that control of his instincts.

"Come on in," Crystal was saying as she opened the door and they walked toward me. They all had the same expression of concern and sadness.

Byron touched my cheek but seemed to have a hard time looking into my eyes. I know he hated that Parker had done this to me.

"Let me see your wrist," he said.

He held it and gently felt the bones and moved it slightly in each direction. Then he manipulated each of my fingers.

"Can you move your fingers?"

"A little, but it hurts," I answered.

"I called Dr. Jamison. He'll be here within a few minutes. I don't want the bone to heal incorrectly, so we can't feed you until he checks it out."

"I can wait," I answered.

"Holly," Byron said, finally looking into my eyes, "I'm so sorry."

"You didn't do anything," I smiled a little.

"Can you tell us what happened?"

So I went through the whole story again. Chris's eyes grew pretty wide and an expression of fear flashed over his face for a second when I told them that Parker ran away from the desire to feed from him. Chris hadn't even seen him. Just heard someone running down the hall.

"I shouldn't have left him alone," Byron sighed almost to himself.

"He shouldn't have gone upstairs," I said using my good hand to reach up and grasp Byron's arm. "I don't think he realized how bad the scent of a human would be."

"Why on Earth would he have gone up there?"

"He wanted to see you and show you he was doing well. The bar was closed, the human customers were gone, and I don't think he thought about the possibility of running into Chris."

"I should have warned him," Byron said obviously angry at himself. "When will I learn to stop keeping things from him?"

Before any of us could answer that, Dr. Jamison was at the door. I think he was surprised to see it was me, a vampire, as a patient. I'd never met him, but knew he was Parker's human doctor. The desire to feed from him was stronger than I expected, but I was able to hold it back. I'd need to feed soon.

"What's the problem?" he asked. Doctor's are good at getting right down to the most important issue.

"I called you to look at her wrist to make sure the bone doesn't need to be set before it heals," Byron answered.

"I don't get many vampire patients," he smiled down at me while checking out the wound on my cheek. "You must be Holly."

"Yes, nice to meet you Dr. Jamison," I answered.

He took my wrist in his hand. "What happened to you?" he asked.

"I fell through a glass table." I couldn't tell him Parker threw me across the room.

"I never heard of a clumsy vampire," he teased. "Where's Parker?"

Was he guessing that this had something to do with Parker or just making what he thought was harmless conversation? He'd been Parker's doctor since Byron adopted him, but probably didn't know he had been changed.

"We'll talk when you're finished with Holly," Byron said. He gave Dr. Jamison a look that let him know there wasn't a quick answer to his question about Parker.

Meanwhile, he'd been exploring the bones in my wrist with the gentle touch of all good doctors. His fingers prodded so lightly, I was surprised that he could tell anything about the bones inside.

"The ulna is broken," he said speaking directly to me. "It's in line, though, and should heal without any problems. I could tell more with an x-ray, but the sun will be rising soon, and we wouldn't be able to move you until tonight. By that time, it should be mostly healed."

"So you think it will be alright?" I asked.

"Yes. I don't foresee any problems. Keep it immobile, but if it still hurts after twenty-four hours or feels weak, call me."

"I will."

"Any other injuries I should see?"

"Her shoulder," Luke said. I'd half forgotten that all of them were there.

I rolled to my side so Dr. Jamison could remove the bandage from my shoulder and have a look.

"Humph." He made that sound that said he was thinking and questioning his options. "It was pretty deep, but healing decently. I think I'll do some stitches just to make sure. I can't very well leave without doing something for you." He winked at me and smiled.

He got the sutures and a syringe out of his bag and gave me a couple shots around the gash which he said would numb the area. The shots hurt, and I wondered if the stitches would have hurt much more, but I didn't say anything. He put in about ten delicate stitches. More than I expected, so I guess that would have hurt more than a few shot.

"You won't need a bandage," he said when he finished. "The stitches will dissolve, but you'll be healed before that. If you want, you can pull them out with tweezers tomorrow."

"Thanks, Doctor," I said when it was obvious that he was finished with me.

"I'll walk upstairs with you and explain what's been going on," Byron said, and they made their way through the door.

Luke, Crystal and Chris stayed with me. Crystal helped me roll onto my back and put an extra pillow next to me so I could rest my wrist on it. It felt good to leave it limp and not try to do anything with it.

"Luke said you'd heal faster after you fed," Chris said as he sat next to me on the bed. "I volunteered for the job."

"No, Chris! Luke can find someone for me."

"I want to."

"When Byron hired you, I made him promise you wouldn't turn into an easy snack for any of us. That includes me."

"Look, little sis," he smiled, "if you were in the hospital and needed a transfusion, I'd donate blood without even thinking about it. This isn't any different."

He had a point, I guessed. We weren't talking about a regular feeding. I needed help healing.

"Are you sure?"

"My neck is all yours," he said as he leaned toward me.

"Your wrist would be easier."

He grinned. "Yeah. Lorna uses my neck."

"The wrist is less intimate. Like they used your wrist to feed Parker." We were both a little embarrassed, so I figured we should get on with it.

I took his wrist in my good hand and gazed into his eyes. "I won't hurt you," I said quietly.

"I know," he answered, but looked a little scared.

I took the fear away while I blocked his pain. He gave me a contented smile and a look that said he loved me. He really did want to be able to help me, but it had to be a little creepy to watch your little sister drink blood from your wrist. I felt a huge swell of love in my heart realizing that my big brother was doing all he could to make me feel better.

Then I bit him and drank until I knew I needed to stop. It was probably more than Lorna had ever taken since she didn't bite him for food. She bit him for the closeness and sexiness.

Once I was finished, I felt stronger, but really sleepy. I licked his wounds away and sat his arm down on the bed, but still held his hand.

"We'll let you sleep," Crystal said.

She and Luke stayed through the feeding, although they had moved as far away as possible. An injured vampire could lose control more easily, so they had to be sure I didn't get carried away while feeding from Chris. I knew watching that had been hard for them and figured they were feeling pretty hungry themselves, so I understood when they left quickly as soon as I finished.

"I'll be asleep in seconds," I answered. "Thanks, Chris, and tell Lorna I took a full feeding so she doesn't take too much."

"No problem." He lightly kissed my injured cheek before leaving.

Alone, I started thinking about Parker. How was he? Were they able to feed him? Did he remember what he'd done? I wanted to run to him and say I loved him and knew he'd be okay, but my injured body wanted to sleep and heal itself.

I couldn't think anymore. It was all too much to let it roll around in my head. Within minutes, I fell into a deep, long sleep.

* * *

Parker and I were walking through a dense forest following a narrow trail that wasn't really a clear path, just matted down undergrowth that lead through the trees. It had probably been made by animals. Humans would have cleared it more.

There was a full moon that shone once in a while through an opening in the leaves and branches overhead. A lot of the area around us, though, was misty and indistinct.

I looked up at Parker and could easily see his bloody fangs and lips, as he smiled at me. I touched my tongue to my own fangs and tasted the rich, warm blood there. Parker leaned down to kiss me and we shared the taste of those humans that lingered in our mouths.

We peeked through the brush at a clearing with an old farmhouse. We watched a man walking toward it from a barn and smelled food cooking. The smell was strong enough that I was sure that human smelled it, too, and looked forward to the meal the woman was cooking inside.

We both inhaled deeply, ignoring the smell of the food, the green forest around us, and a wood fire burning inside the house. We relished the scent of the human that would be our next meal.

With our vampire speed, we broke through the door. I grabbed the man and threw him to the floor. Parker went for the woman and I caught a glimpse of him pinning her against a wall.

Our speed was such that neither of them had any hint that they were being attacked. Their faces froze in an expression of the sudden fear that we created. Within seconds they'd gone from peacefully preparing an evening meal to abject terror as they realized they were about to die.

Their screams rang through the night as we plunged our fangs into their necks and fed. We drank deeply and I couldn't get enough blood fast enough. I was taking it so fast that it overfilled my mouth and ran down my chin and his neck. Still I kept drinking.

The blood slowed, but I wanted more. I pulled out my fangs and bit him again on the other side of his neck, deeper, trying to find a new supply, but his veins were empty.

I licked the blood from his neck, but that still wasn't enough. Pulling back I felt a deep rage building in me, blaming him for not giving me all I wanted.

My rage at him spiked and I ripped his shirt open, gripped the flesh of his chest and tore through it with my bare hands. I plucked his still heart from his dead body and bit into it, lapping up any drops I could find.

Parker was standing over me laughing. I dropped the heart on the floor, stood up, and ran my tongue over his lips to steal a taste of his prey. He licked the man's blood from my chin. Parker grabbed my hand, laughing, and we ran off back to the forest.

The dream changed and I was stretched out on the dirt floor of a cave. I had woken to a noise, and realized it was a scream. I looked over to see Parker flat on his back, eyes staring blankly at nothing, with a wooden stake sticking out of his chest. It was his scream that had awakened me.

The scent of humans filled the cavern and someone held me down. I struggled to get away, but more hands grabbed my arms, shoulders, and legs. I heard my own screams and felt the pain of the stake that plunged into my heart.

I was covered in sweat and my heart was racing when I really woke in my own bed. The dream seemed so real that I could still taste that man's blood in my mind.

I spread my fingers across my chest to make sure there was no stake sticking out of it. Then I lay on my back breathing deeply, trying to calm my pulse, and holding my heart to assure myself that it was still intact.

Was that dream a reflection of the stories Crystal had told me about the past, or some horrible prediction of the future Parker and I could have together? Either way, I wanted the memory of it gone. I was afraid I'd never be able to feed again without visions of that bloodthirst jumping into my head.

Worst of all, though, was the realization that my dream vision could come true for Parker if Byron couldn't help him get control. Seeing Parker lose it when he got a whiff of Chris and Sarita made me see how helpless he was when bloodthirst hit him.

That's what the dream was, an acknowledgement of my fear that we may not be able to help Parker. He may not be able to learn to control his predator instincts. We may still lose him no matter what we did.

Chapter 14

Constance, Bartholomew and Samuel, the three oldest, strongest, and most experienced of the Vampire Assembly, had a serious problem. The phone call from Charles when he claimed that Byron's son had become bloodthirsty had caused much discussion and controversy.

Constance had kept it to herself for several hours while she thought over his every word and the ramifications of what needed to be done if Charles was telling the truth. Charles had been right that the law required death for anyone that harbored a bloodthirsty vampire, but he seemed to forget that Constance was the law.

She was the head of the Vampire Assembly and, even though they discussed and argued over every issue, Constance made the final decisions. There was no provision for voting, or compromising. She created the Assembly centuries before and her word was law until she chose to step down.

In this situation, Charles's actions were so obviously a plot to destroy Byron that she'd have to proceed carefully. She didn't want to kill Byron, one of her strongest supporters, and Charles knew it. But, if Charles's story was true, how could she *not* kill him?

Constance had to take this to the Assembly, but she also had to treat it with some discretion. Her closest advisors and the strongest, except for herself, were Samuel and Bartholomew. They were the ones she'd taken with her to deal with Charles at Nibble. Like her, they knew Charles couldn't be trusted, but they also were equally determined not to let a bloodthirsty vampire survive.

"This is Byron we're talking about," Bartholomew said. "He has strongly supported us from the beginning. We have to be careful to not accuse him falsely of harboring a bloodthirsty vampire."

"Of course," Samuel added, "but we also can't ignore it. Others would see it as favoritism, and our authority and ability to enforce the laws would be jeopardized."

"Is it possible Charles was lying?" Bartholomew asked Constance.

"Anything's possible, but I can't think of what it would gain him. He obviously wanted us to seize Parker and punish Byron," Constance answered. "And he made sure to remind me of the punishment for hiding bloodthirst."

"Rather ironic that it's the very crime Charles is guilty of," Bartholomew said with a mild disgust.

"True," Constance said. "But we know that Charles abducted Parker and held him for several days before Byron rescued him. The most logical conclusion is that Charles changed him in the old ways to purposely create bloodthirst."

"To what end?" Samuel asked looking doubtful about Constance's conclusion.

"To punish Byron," Constance answered making it sound like the answer was obvious. "He's always seen Byron as a rival, but now Byron's ruined the plans to gain power that Charles has worked on for decades."

"And destroyed two bloodthirst clubs while doing away with most of his trusted followers," Bartholomew added. "Knowing Charles, he's probably determined to devastate Byron, Rule the Night, and all those he cares about. Charles can be ruthless."

"That all makes sense," Samuel said, "but I still don't think we can ignore the situation with Byron and his son. We have to enforce our laws."

"No, we can't ignore it," Constance said. "But I'm not ready to make a final decision without talking to Byron, and this is too important for a phone call. I'm going to Rule the Night to check the situation for myself. I want to see this young one and assess his condition."

Samuel frowned at Constance. "We wouldn't want it to appear that your relationship with Byron influenced your judgment."

Constance's anger flared and radiated through the room. "It is none of your concern how my judgments *appear*, Samuel. You should consider carefully how your *words* appear."

"I apologize, Constance," Samuel said. Somehow, though, Constance couldn't quite believe that that his apology was sincere.

"It's close to dawn," Constance said. "I'll go see Byron tonight. Bartholomew, I'd like to speak to you alone."

Her words clearly dismissed Samuel, so he left them, but not happily.

"I'd like you to travel with me to Rule the Night," she said as soon as Samuel was gone.

"I would be glad to," Bartholomew answered.

"Your opinion is valuable to me," Constance continued. "It wasn't Samuel's place to mention how my judgment might appear, but he was right. Everyone knows Byron and I have worked closely for centuries, and it would be easy for them to think my decision favored him."

"If we're lucky, Charles exaggerated the situation and there will be no problem."

Constance's eyes narrowed and her mouth formed a stern line. "If there was no problem, I think Byron would have already reported that to us. I'm afraid that no word from him means there's something he doesn't want to report until he tries to solve it himself."

* * *

After the horrible dream about Parker and me killing the humans in the farm house, I didn't know if I'd go back to sleep or not. I must have, though, because I was waking up again.

I turned my head to look at the clock on the nightstand, but instead saw Byron gazing at me from a chair that had been pulled next to my bed. I couldn't help smiling at him, but he didn't smile back. In fact, he looked like he was near tears.

"How do you feel?" he asked quietly.

"Okay, I think," I answered. "My wrist feels good." I gently circled it around and flexed my fingers.

"I'm so sorry," he said with deep concern in his voice.

He looked so sad and so miserable. I sat up crossing my legs under me and reached out for Byron's hand. He held on to it for a second, but then leaned forward and hugged me really tight.

"I don't know if I can save him," he whispered in my ear with so much despair in his voice I felt tears fill my eyes.

I held on to him. If Byron was this upset, Parker must have been really bad after they carried him to his room. Did I want to know what had happened? No, I really didn't. But I needed to.

"Tell me, Byron," I whispered.

He pulled away from me to settle back in the chair and shook his head.

"I'm sorry I'm being so emotional," he said steadying his voice. "I just hate to see you getting hurt."

"Stop hiding things from me." I didn't yell at him, but I wanted to. "Tell me what happened in Parker's room this morning."

He looked at me without saying anything for several minutes, then rubbed those lines between his eyes.

"I was so sure I could help him find control," he practically whispered turning his eyes away from mine. "But he's getting worse."

"Worse?"

"He wouldn't stop fighting us. He broke TJ's nose and kicked me, bruising my ribs."

I gasped. TJ and Byron were two really powerful vampires. For Parker to have done that, he must have been delirious, still in such a rage that he didn't know what he was doing.

"We had to tie him down. Lorna brought him a donor, and the feeding finally calmed him some, but we had to leave him tied."

"Oh, God." My face fell into my hands and I sat there completely numb. I didn't know what to think or what to say.

"I haven't given up," Byron said with more determination than I thought he was really feeling.

"How could Charles be so evil?" I eventually asked.

Byron opened his mouth to answer, but the knock on my door stopped him. It was Crystal. She opened the door without waiting for one of us to answer. The look on her face scared me.

"Constance and Bartholomew are in your office," Crystal said from the doorway.

Byron looked into my eyes and still didn't stay anything. I couldn't read the look on his face, but at least some of it was a deep fear. After taking a slow breath, he walked past Crystal heading for the stairs.

Crystal looked toward me with such despair and fear on her face, my stomach churned and I thought my heart would stop. I understood her look. If the highest authorities in the vampire world bothered to show up unannounced, it would not be good news.

I knew Byron hadn't told them what kind of shape Parker was in. It's not that he didn't plan on ever telling them, but he needed time to prove that Parker would be able to overcome bloodthirst.

The reality, though, was that the Assembly rules didn't provide such time. We all knew that Parker might not be able to find control unless he was given decades. Decades of uncontrollable killing. The Assembly would not let that happen.

As Crystal walked out of my room without finding anything to say to me, the reality hit, and I started to move. I dressed as fast as I could, pulled my hair back in a pony tail because I didn't have time to even try brushing the bed-head out of it, and I ran.

I got to Parker's room within a few seconds, but still had time on the way to fret about what I might see when I got there. The sun had set. Would Parker be ranting and raving about feeding? Was he still tied to his bed so he couldn't attack the nearest human?

What would the Assembly do? They could make the decision to execute him and take him away with them. They could decide to kill him immediately as he fought them and struggled against the bindings that held him.

Within minutes, Parker could be dead and there'd be nothing any of us could do to save him. That's probably why they showed up without any warning. Parker would have no chance to run.

I burst through the door to Parker's suite and was shocked to see him and Quinton walking into the living room from the bedroom. Parker was dressed in jeans and a tee shirt and looked like his normal self.

Parker froze where he stood and gazed into my eyes. I kept walking to him not even glancing at Quinton. Fear, questions, sorrow, it all showed on Parker's face as I approached.

All I could do, though, was reach up to put my arms around his neck and kiss him. Parker was so surprised he tried to pull away from me a little as our lips met, but that didn't last. He kissed me back with all the love I knew he had for me.

We broke the kiss, but continued to hug.

"I love you," I whispered into his ear.

He pulled away and held my face in his hands. "How could you? After what I did?"

"Do you remember saying that you didn't want to hurt me?"

"The whole thing's like ... like I was watching someone else. Are you okay?"

"I'm fine." My mind was thinking, *The hell with how I am. Do you know the Assembly's here?*

"Has Byron called?" I asked Quinton.

"Crystal warned us when she was on her way to get Byron."

"Good." Then I looked back to Parker. "They may want to talk to you."

"I know," he nodded. "I'll talk to them."

We all three sensed them outside the door. I wanted time to talk to Parker, to assure him, and to get some idea from Quinton if he thought things would go well or not. Parker looked like his normal self to me, but he had to be getting hungry. How long would his calmness last?

Quinton opened the door, and I swallowed hard watching Byron, Crystal, Constance, and Bartholomew walk in. We all greeted each other very politely with half-smiles, but I could feel the questions and fear radiate through the room.

Inside my head I was screaming. How could we pretend to be so polite and friendly when we all knew that they could kill Parker at any time? Maybe Byron had been able to talk them out of it. Maybe Parker and I could still run for it.

With that thought came the memory of my dream. My heart felt like it stopped and I had to swallow hard again. That was the moment that I knew I'd do it.

I'd run away with him if we had to. I knew I'd kill *for* Parker. Would I kill *with* him? Would I be willing to let my own hidden beast out to be with him? If it came right down to it and the only other option was watching him die, my answer was *Yes,* I would.

"We'd like to talk to Parker alone," Constance said to the crowded room.

"That's okay," Parker answered nodding toward Byron.

I knew Byron hated leaving Parker alone with them, but he kept his face almost perfectly blank. It was only the tiny hint of fear in his eyes that gave him away.

My face, however, announced to everyone how scared I was. My eyes were huge while my brows were drawn together and my lips were rolled in and clamped between my teeth. I hated this so much I thought I might explode.

Parker gave me a forced smile and squeezed my hand. He was trying to make me feel better, but nothing was going to accomplish that. How could I feel better about leaving him alone with the very people who were prepared to execute him?

We all left, but we didn't go very far.

Sitting on the couches in the common area, my mind flashed back to the time in the hospital waiting for Chris to get out of appendix surgery. He was about fourteen and hadn't told Mom and Dad how much his side was hurting until he couldn't stand up anymore. They had rushed him in to operate right from the emergency room, and we were afraid he might die.

Obviously, the scare with Chris had turned out well. I couldn't shake the feeling that this time, my waiting to hear the fate of someone I loved might have a very different outcome.

Surprisingly, the Assembly's questioning of Parker didn't take as long as I was afraid it would. Constance and Bartholomew came down the hall toward us after only about ten minutes.

We all stood, anxious to hear what they were going to tell us. If they had decided they couldn't let him live, would they even give us a chance to say goodbye? Had they already killed him? I was shaking. So afraid that I'd never hold or even see Parker again.

Constance spoke directly to Byron, but we all hung on her every word.

"Parker handled himself very honorably," Constance said with a tone that seemed to be telling Byron to be proud of him.

I felt my heart skip a beat and my stomach clench. Was that an old fashioned way of saying that he died with honor? Died without getting hysterical and fighting them? I couldn't stand much more of this.

"He admits he has practically no control," she continued.

She spoke of him in present tense. If he was dead, wouldn't she have spoken of the past? I wanted to shake her and scream at her to stop all the crap and tell us if he was still alive, or if they were going to let him live much longer.

"He is in such a state that I would have no problem ordering his execution, except for the fact that none of this was his doing. Bloodthirst was imposed upon him to punish you. Charles is the guilty party in this, not Parker."

She's going to let him live! The relief poured through me, and I felt myself breathe again.

"But, we can't allow him to continue killing."

She looked at Byron with an expression of profound grief. The relief that I'd felt for that short few seconds, drained away. How could my emotions flip and flop, back and forth, from despair to relief so fast and so many times in only a few seconds?

"I'm going to give you some time, Byron. A week. If he hasn't shown some improvement in the next week, we will have to step in. He wants to control his instincts, which is a good sign, and I know that if anyone can train him, it's you. But we can't let this go on indefinitely."

"A week isn't very long," Byron said with more strength in his voice than I ever could have pulled together. I was a wreck. If I'd tried to speak I don't think anything but a whining scream would have come out of my mouth.

"A week for *some* improvement. I don't expect him to become a fully trained, unrestricted vampire in that time. He told me what happened with the human named Chris who he considers to be a good friend. Perhaps if Parker was exposed again to his scent, only in a controlled way, he could learn to tolerate the proximity of humans. That would be a positive indication that he is trainable."

"Chris is Holly's brother and Lorna's human lover. I couldn't endanger him."

"Of course not. Parker would have to be restrained until you could determine if their friendship influenced his control."

"We'll try," Byron said.

There wasn't much more any of us could say. Constance told us she'd check on his progress in a week. Did that mean she'd show up unannounced again? Probably.

Byron walked Constance and Bartholomew back upstairs leaving Quinton, Crystal, and me standing there staring at each other.

"I'm relieved," Quinton said once they were gone.

"Will a week be enough, Quinton?" I asked with panic still on the edge of my voice. "Do you think that Parker can improve in that time?"

"He wants to," he answered. "He told me he's disgusted with himself for the way he wanted to feed on Chris and Sarita. And how he hurt you. It may be what he needs to continue fighting the bloodthirst."

"You really think so?"

"We know how twisted Charles is, and he tried to teach Parker to be the same, to be proud of the powerful predator inside him. I think Parker's really seen the truth ..." Quinton shook his head slightly as he thought and looked away from me. "The predator in us doesn't care who it hurts, doesn't care about anyone or anything but its own hunger. I think we've all had to learn that before we could fight it."

I got the feeling that Quinton was talking about more than Parker. I wanted to ask him, but that just wasn't the time.

"I hope you're right," was all I said. Quinton's eyes met mine, and I saw a lot of sadness there.

"We should check on Parker," Crystal said quietly.

Chapter 15

A week felt like such a short time. Parker hadn't made any improvement so far, and it seemed to me that he would need much more than only one week.

But maybe Constance knew what she was doing. Demanding progress in a short time might make Parker try harder and get more determined to reach deep inside himself to fight bloodthirst.

Not that I thought Parker wasn't trying. I knew he was. He didn't want to kill humans anymore than the rest of us did, but Charles had taught his instincts that killing was the only way to be a vampire.

Only a week. But sometimes the added pressure of a time limit could make us reach for a seemingly unattainable goal and make it. It happened all the time in sports, didn't it? The last minute come-from-behind win when a team seemed to have lost, gave us hope through almost any game. Could Parker pull it off?

I didn't know. I had hope. I had faith in his ability to find control over his instincts, but hope and faith in someone weren't always enough.

None of the really young vampires of the past were able to overcome bloodthirst. Even many of the older ones had a really hard time. What were the odds that Parker could do it when so many others had failed? Honestly, not good.

All these thoughts and many more raced through my head as we walked toward Parker's room, yet a part of me felt strangely numb. I think it was the part of my mind that would normally come to some conclusion, or find an answer to a problem.

But there wasn't any clear solution to the crisis we were attempting to deal with. Parker would find the strength to overcome bloodthirst or he wouldn't. We could try to help him, but the bottom line was that he had to find the control he needed within himself.

That's what caused my numbness. No matter what, we were essentially helpless. We couldn't call a doctor to give Parker a certain medicine that would heal him.

I found myself reminded of the black plague that had killed about half the population of Europe in the Middle Ages. There was no cure, no treatment. All people could do was try to make the victims more comfortable as they died.

But a few, very few, surprisingly survived that horrible disease. Something in them gave them the ability to overcome it, and they actually got better and lived. I prayed that Parker could find something in himself that would enable him to do the same.

"How ya' doin', man?" Quinton said as we walked into Parker's room.

He was sitting on the couch with his feet up on the coffee table, a wooden one Byron had moved in from somewhere since the old one shattered with the force of my body flying across the room. Probably shouldn't think about that.

"Good," Parker answered quietly. "But the Indians are losing." Parker jutted out his chin toward the baseball game on the TV. I got the idea he'd rather talk about something other than himself.

When he noticed me, he grinned and got off the couch. He wrapped his arms around my waist, pulled me close, and kissed me. My arms went around his neck and I kissed him back. Not a big, hard, passionate kiss, though. We gave each other kisses that said *I love you*.

Keeping one arm around my waist, he leaned away from me and took Crystal's hand. "Good to see you, too, Crystal." Then he kissed her cheek.

"Parker, how was it with Constance?" I had to know. I really would have liked to talk about anything else, but I had to know.

"Let's sit down." We walked to the couch without him letting go of me. All four of us sat down. Quinton and Crystal in the chairs, while Parker and I sat next to each other on the couch. Parker moved his arm across my shoulders.

"I was really scared of being alone with her," he said mainly to me, but actually talking to all of us.

"Can't blame you for that," Quinton said. Parker looked over at Quinton.

"But she turned out to be really nice. She mainly wanted to know how I felt when I fed and she seemed to understand. I think her giving me a week is pretty fair."

"We wondered if she told you that," Crystal said.

"Did she tell you about bringing in Chris to get you used to a human's scent?" Again, I asked because I had to know. Deep down the whole business of using Chris scared the hell out of me.

"I don't like that part," Parker shook his head like he was thinking about refusing to do it.

"You'll be restrained," Quinton said. "No way we'll let you hurt Chris."

"I know, but I'm not sure I want him to see me like that." His voice was quiet.

"That's because you want to control it," Quinton said. "If you didn't, you wouldn't care who saw the bloodthirst."

"I guess," Parker shrugged. I wasn't so sure he was convinced, so I reached up to hold his hand that was resting on my shoulder.

After I attacked Parker, I was embarrassed as hell that I couldn't control myself. I never wanted to show that to anyone ever again. Maybe Constance knew what she was doing more than I realized. Maybe Parker's embarrassment would help him find control.

"I don't know what Byron's thinking," Quinton continued, "but I think we should bring Chris down here tonight."

"Not 'till after I feed." I could hear a little panic creeping into Parker's voice. He really wanted to give this every chance to work, and I was thrilled to hear that.

"You getting hungry?"

"Yeah," he nodded.

"I'll call TJ." Quinton speed dialed his cell and only spoke to TJ for a few seconds. "He has someone picked out," Quinton said when he hung up. "He'll have her here in a few minutes."

Parker had a silent apology on his face when he looked toward me. Of course, with his arm around my shoulders, that look was only a few inches away.

"I guess that's time for you and Crystal to leave," he whispered.

"Can I come back when they bring Chris in?"

He shook his head. "I'd rather you didn't. I'm sorry, but I just don't know how it's going to go." He looked so intense and scared.

Quinton and Crystal were just a few feet away from us, but staring into Parker's eyes with our faces only inches apart made me feel like we were completely alone in the universe. We hadn't had much time alone, and being this close to him triggered those feelings of how much I longed for him.

If we had been alone, I think I would have jumped him right then and there. He must have seen those feelings on my face because his gaze heated up and his arm tightened around my shoulders. I knew he was thinking the same thing.

As much as I didn't want to, I had to pull my eyes away from his and get back to the conversation we were in the middle of. I looked down at my hand resting on my thigh and forced myself to visualize that scared look he'd had the moment before.

"You know they won't let you hurt Chris. Tell me what's bothering you." I was able to look back at him.

Parker reached his free arm around my waist and pulled me against him resting his cheek against the top of my head. It felt so good for him to hold me like that.

He almost whispered, "Constance made it pretty clear that this is my last chance. If I can't control myself around Chris ..."

"Don't say it! Don't even think it!" I pulled away so I could see him again. "We won't give up on you. I don't care what Constance says or how much time she says we should give you."

Now I could hear the panic in my own voice. Did Parker think we'd all just let Constance stroll in here and kill him? I wouldn't and I knew Byron wouldn't let her do it either.

"I know, sweetheart, I know." He hugged me again. "Besides, this will work. I'll be fine with Chris. It'll all work out."

What a moment for Quinton's phone to ring. I can't really say it interrupted, though, because I had nothing to say. At least nothing I could find words for.

I wanted to tell Parker that I knew he was right and he'd be fine and we'd carry on with our normal vampire lives. We'd be able to feed in the bar together and live together forever like we'd planned.

But I also wanted to tell him that I had a plan if it didn't work. As much as I hated that dream of the two of us feeding and killing, I knew that I'd run away with Parker and help him do what he had to do. If my only choice was watching him kill or watching him die, I'd take watching him kill without a second thought.

That's what I most wanted to say, but I couldn't say it in front of Quinton and Crystal. I couldn't let them know that I had a plan for us to run. And I couldn't tell Parker, yet. Not until he had every chance to find the control he needed.

"I believe in you, Parker," I whispered back while Quinton talked to TJ. "You're right. It'll work."

* * *

Parker sat quietly on his bed and leaned against the headboard. He gazed across the room at the picture of himself with Holly that hung next to the bookcase. Their faces showed all the love they had for each other.

It was a reflection of the unconditional love his parents had felt for each other and for him. The love he found again with Holly. The picture gave him hope for their future, but sometimes he couldn't stand to look at it because he didn't know if that future could ever become reality.

The straps Quinton used to restrain Parker were made from seatbelt fabric. Even vampire strength couldn't rip through them. He buckled one around Parker's chest holding his arms tight against his body. The next one went around his waist and forearms. Another around his thighs, and the last one bound his calves.

Parker leaned forward so Quinton could access the chain at the back of the strap around his waist. Quinton pulled it through the slats on the headboard and fastened it to the hook screwed into the wall.

"Too tight?" Quinton asked when he finished.

200

"It's good," Parker answered.

They hadn't said anything during the process of restraining Parker. They both hated that it had to be done this way, but it created the safest situation for everyone involved.

Parker had healed completely from his enforced exposure to the sun and had gotten strong enough that he was able to injure them when they tried to hold him down. Eventually, someone was going to get seriously hurt, or they would be forced to hurt him. Tying him down was the only way to keep them all safe.

They both scented TJ and a human woman outside the door. Parker tried not to breathe too deeply, but still the smell of human made his gums tingle as his fangs started to descend.

He tried to concentrate on her life instead of her blood. He mentally told himself that he didn't want this woman to die. She deserved to live.

He envisioned himself feeding enough to touch his hunger and then stopping to lick away her wounds. He tried to convince himself that would be enough.

That monstrous beast inside, though, was already contradicting him. It was saying that he had to drink until there was nothing left. He had to drain her, or he'd still be hungry. He'd be hungry forever if he stopped before she was dead.

Holly told him the beast lied, and the hunger would be gone if he stopped. The hunger told him that it wasn't true. Holly was the liar. Would Holly lie to him? As her scent reached him, the hunger wanted her blood, all her blood. Parker wanted it, too, because he was that beast.

Quinton watched Parker as TJ walked into the room with the woman. As usual he led her like she had no idea where she was or what she was doing. She'd never remember a thing.

But Quinton wasn't even thinking about her. He watched Parker's reaction. Watched his eyes glaze over as he stared at the woman. Watched his lip seem to swell over his growing fangs. Parker leaned his body forward as far as he could and his nostrils flared to breathe her scent deeper into his body.

Quinton stepped in front of him and caught the anger radiating from his eyes. Parker did not like having his view of the woman disrupted and he couldn't move far enough to look around Quinton.

"Are you trying to fight it?" he asked.

"Yeah," Parker answered, but Quinton could tell he was still distracted from everything else except the smell of the woman's blood.

"Beat the hunger back, Parker. Get it set in your mind *now* that you'll be able to stop. Do it for Holly."

"I'm trying, Q! Get the hell out of my way!" Parker screamed out at him.

Quinton stepped aside knowing that this was going to be just like every other feeding. If only there was some way to help, he'd do it. He'd wracked his brain to think of anything that might make a difference.

All he could think, though, was the same thing he'd been thinking since Charles took Parker. Someday, he'd kill Charles. Someday, really soon, Charles would pay for what he'd done to Parker and how he'd treated Holly, and Quinton would be the one to make him pay.

Chapter 16

Crystal stepped into Byron's office to leave him a note about ordering for the bar. She stopped in her tracks when she realized that he was sitting behind his desk with some kind of paperwork spread out in front of him.

"You didn't go down for Parker's feeding?"

"I had some stuff to do here," Byron answered without looking up.

"Are you taking Chris down?"

"I don't know."

Byron hadn't looked up at Crystal, but she kept staring at him. Normally, Byron would have gotten up from his desk and given her a kiss, or at least a hug.

"What's wrong?" she asked.

"Just busy," Byron answered finally looking at her. His eyes immediately flashed back to the paper on the desk.

Crystal went to him and leaned down to kiss him. Byron kissed her back, but it was a quick peck, not his usual at all.

Crystal looked at his profile while he concentrated on his desktop. At least he seemed to be concentrating on the desktop. She had a feeling there was much more on his mind.

"Okay, Byron," she finally said as she crossed her arms over her chest and leaned one hip against the side of the desk. "You haven't seen Parker since Constance left, have you?"

He glanced up at her for a second, then his eyes dropped back to the desk again. "I told you I'm busy."

"You have never in your life been too busy for Parker. You've never been too busy to take care of any of us that needed you. What are you thinking? Please, Byron, tell me."

He finally looked at her and held her gaze. He looked exhausted, sad, and almost lonely. Then he reached up to take her hand.

"I'm having a difficult time dealing with Parker lately. I need some time to think." Byron's voice was very quiet, but also very serious.

"Did Constance say something?"

"Nothing that she didn't say to everyone."

"Then what? Of course the situation with Parker is difficult. What do you need time to think about?"

"He's bloodthirsty."

"Yes."

"I've spent centuries fighting against bloodthirst. I can't even remember how many I've executed for the Assembly. I've never regretted one of them. They killed humans and had to be stopped. Any vampire that wouldn't or couldn't control their instincts deserved to die."

"But now it's Parker."

"My son." His eyes showed the anguish he'd been living with.

"What are you saying, Byron?" There was fear in Crystal's voice.

"Does he deserve death any less than the others?"

"Yes! Like you said, he's your son."

Byron took a deep breath and pushed it out slowly. He didn't want to fight with Crystal because he'd been fighting with himself for days.

"I can turn him over to the Assembly, or I can take him somewhere into hiding."

"You can't turn him in," Crystal practically shouted with more hysteria than volume. "You can't send Parker out to die." She felt his thumb begin to gently stroke the back of her hand.

"So the choice is to hide him. Keep him locked away, continue to tie him down to feed, make sure no human has any contact with him, and no vampire could be allowed to know where he is, because they'd turn him in.

"Then in fifty to a hundred years, he should find enough control to feed on his own. Maybe. How long do I keep him prisoner? How long can he keep his sanity in such isolation? How long before he escapes and kills again?"

"I don't know how long, but I know it's too soon to give up."

"I haven't given up." He pulled Crystal onto his lap and wrapped his arms around her shoulders. "I'm just facing the reality that the time may come when we have to."

"That's like giving yourself permission to fail."

"I can't pretend that Parker has a good chance of overcoming this. I saw too many like him. They all failed."

"Parker has so many to help him, so many of us who love him. None of those others had that."

"I don't know if that will make any difference."

"Don't let Parker get the idea you've given up. Take Chris to him." Crystal's tone was almost pleading. "Show him you believe in him. It might help him to know that."

"It might."

"It breaks my heart to see him like that," Crystal whispered, and Byron noticed a tear roll down her cheek. He kissed it away.

* * *

My bed felt like it didn't want me in it. I rolled from my right side to my left, from my back to my stomach, and no position was comfortable enough to sleep. The pillow was even worse, like someone emptied out the feathers and filled it with cement.

The sun had been up for almost two hours and I would normally be lost in my deep, vampire sleep, but not today. My thoughts kept flipping from one thing to another, but all the flips centered on one thing. Parker.

I worried about his bloodthirst, the Assembly coming after him, his reaction to Chris. Was he improving at all? Would he find control over the monster inside him? Could I stick to my conviction of running away with him?

Those thoughts had distracted me while trying to serve drinks to customers all night. Crystal and Luke had tried to get me thinking about something else while we worked, but nothing helped for long.

Chris never came to the bar and we never heard anything from Byron, so I kind of assumed things didn't go well. If Parker had been able to control it around Chris, he would have come running to the bar to tell me the good news. They were all trying to protect me, but I was much more interested in protecting Parker.

Byron had stayed with him all night, so I didn't even go in to see him. I figured he and Byron needed time to talk, but mostly I was just too upset. I didn't want Parker to see me on the verge of tears. I wanted him to stay positive. If only I could stay positive.

Once more I threw myself to my back and lay there with my hands holding my head like I could squeeze all the thoughts away. It was hopeless. I wasn't going to sleep anytime soon, so I got up and walked around my room.

Under all the worries and what-ifs, I realized there was one basic issue. I missed Parker. I missed his face, his voice, his laugh, and his arms around me. He was my best friend, I loved him with all my heart, and I'd hardly spent any time with him for weeks. I needed to see him.

I threw my nightshirt and boy shorts onto the bed and walked naked into the closet. I now had a really nice wardrobe with all kinds of choices, but I went for my old fall-back of jeans and the first t-shirt my hand reached, a deep rose and white stripped one.

It didn't matter what I wore. I just needed to be decent. The client rooms were always full these days, and some of them might still be awake and in the common room, but I didn't even bother to look in the mirror or try to control my hair.

All I could think about was that Byron or one of the guards was sitting in Parker's room watching him sleep. I wanted that to be me. I needed to sit there gazing at his peaceful face. I just needed to be in the same room with him or I might go insane.

The feeling was that strong, like I could lose my mind if I didn't see him. I was so tired of everyone else spending more time with Parker than me. I should be taking care of him and helping him.

We were in love and we planned to spend our lives together. My stomach clenched as I realized that his life may be much shorter than we'd originally thought. He might only have days left to live. I needed to spend those days with him.

I didn't bother to knock, but Byron heard me open the door to Parker's suite. He met me in the living room.

"How is he?" I asked.

"Sound asleep, as you should be," Byron answered.

"I can't sleep. I feel like I may never sleep again."

"Do you want to talk?"

"No. I want to sit with Parker. You've hardly slept in weeks, so I'll stay with him while you go get some rest."

"Holly, you're not strong enough to control him."

"You said he's sound asleep. What's to control?"

"What if he tries to leave his room again?"

"He won't. Besides, I can call you."

"Are you sure?"

"Yes, I'm sure. Go hold Crystal, get some sleep, and take the time to not worry about Parker or me."

"That's very tempting."

"You're dead on your feet. Go!"

"Well, he has been sleeping through the day and not waking until it's almost dark. I guess there's really no good reason for you not to stay. But, if you need anything, call me right away. If you can't stay awake, I'll come back."

Byron left with less argument than I expected. He must have been a lot more worn out than I realized.

I went into Parker's room and sat in the big, overstuffed chair Byron just left. He'd pulled it up close to the bottom of the bed, and I could tell from the dents in the feather comforter that he'd had his feet up on the corner of the mattress. I had to push the chair a little closer to get my feet there.

I couldn't see Parker's face from the bottom of the bed, and I needed to see him. I scooted the chair to the side, right next to his bedside table. I folded my legs under me and sat with my hands in my lap.

A tiny smile grew on my lips as I stared at him. Sleeping on his side left half his face buried in the pillow, but the half that I could see calmed me. Parker's face, so familiar, yet somehow different.

When Byron changed me, Sarita mentioned how I had changed physically. How becoming a vampire had enhanced my appearance. I could see that, now, in Parker.

His features weren't different, just slightly enhanced. His bone structure was stronger, his lips a little fuller, and the stubble of his beard heavier. He looked even more masculine, older. There was nothing about that eighteen-year-old face that said he was still a boy. He was all man.

I could hear his periodic breathing and the beat of his heart. His scent gently wafted to me and I inhaled deeply. He smelled so good. Not so long ago, I'd stood next to his bed and hungered for his human blood. I had to run from his room that night to keep from devouring him.

The longing I felt now wasn't for the taste of his blood. I longed to crawl into that bed and make love to him. I wanted to sleep every day in his arms and wake to his face showing his love for me.

I wanted the life together that the two of us had planned.

Enjoying the thoughts of how happy we intended to be, I realized that Parker was gazing back at me. His dreamy eyes held mine and I somehow had the feeling that he was reading my mind. I smiled and leaned in a little toward him.

"It really is you. I thought I was dreaming," Parker said with a still sleepy voice.

"It's me."

"Byron's letting you guard me?"

"He was exhausted. I told him to get some sleep."

Parker turned his face farther into the pillow so he wasn't looking at me anymore. "I think he was upset about how I reacted to Chris."

"What happened?" My stomach clenched as I imagined the worst.

"I couldn't control it. I smelled his blood and I tried to get at him. Byron had to send him back to Lorna's room." Then he buried his face completely and mumbled, "It's hopeless."

He sounded so miserable. I moved from the chair to sit next to him on the bed and rested my hand on his shoulder.

"We haven't given up on you, so don't give up on yourself," I whispered, leaning down to him. I kissed his cheek. "You just need more time."

Parker turned and looked at me. We were just inches apart, and my gaze moved from his eyes to his lips. I wanted those lips.

The look in his eyes told me he felt the same thing, and we both moved toward each other into a sweet kiss. It was only seconds before that kiss became more passionate and I stopped breathing.

Never breaking the kiss, Parker rolled slightly onto his back putting his arms around me and pulling me down against him. The blanket got pushed down to his waist as he pulled out his arms, and I found myself pressed against the bare muscles of his chest and abs.

My hands roamed over those muscles and his hands caressed my back and slid under my t-shirt. Both hands stopped in the middle of my back when he realized I hadn't bothered putting on a bra.

"Shit, Holly," he gasped against my lips.

I sat up and stared down at him. The question was in his eyes, but there was no question about it in my mind. Without thinking twice, I pulled the t-shirt over my head and threw it toward the chair I'd been sitting in.

"Damn," was the only thing that came from his lips as he reached up to pull me back down against his chest.

I hadn't gone there to have sex with Parker, but maybe something in my sub-conscious had intended that to happen all along. I didn't know.

All I knew was that I wanted him and all the old reasons not to be together were gone. I wasn't dangerous to him anymore. We were both vampires and loved each other more than anything. On top of all that was the subconscious thought that he might be dead very soon.

It was early afternoon before I woke in Parker's arms and I was the one that thought I was dreaming. He smiled down at me, and gently kissed me.

"Have you been awake long?" I asked.

"I didn't go to sleep. Just watched you," he smiled.

I stroked his cheek and he held me tighter.

"No matter what happens ..." I started to say.

"No, Holly," he shook his head. "I don't want to talk about all that. I just want to hold you and pretend everything's okay."

"I know, but I have to tell you while we're alone and I have the chance. I won't let them take you."

"Holly, please don't ..." Parker started to pull away from me.

"Listen to me." I pulled him back and held him close. "I've been planning how we can run away. We'll be together and I'll help you." He was shaking his head again as I talked. "Parker, we can hide out until you get better. I know you can do it if we're together."

"Babe, this isn't going to go away just because we want it to. I'm not like Charles and the others you knew at Nibble. I'm not bloodthirsty by choice, and I can't control it. Charles made me bloodthirsty and everyone knows that I'm too young to find any control over that hunger."

"No! Byron helped others find control and he thinks you can do it."

"Holly, we can't lie to ourselves." His voice was so quiet and sad. "I think even Byron is losing hope. You haven't seen him in here. Last night, the look on his face ..." Parker shook his head and his expression was almost desperate. "He looked like he was saying goodbye to me. He's already thinking of me as dead."

"That's not true! You just need more time!" I felt a tear run down my cheek as I shouted at him. He hugged me and stroked my hair.

"Okay. Please don't cry. Maybe he hasn't given up, but he knows I really haven't gotten any better. Maybe you're right and I need more time."

"Parker, promise me you won't let Constance take you. Promise me we'll run away."

"If they catch us, they'll execute you, too, for helping me. I can't let you do that."

"How am I supposed to live without you? The best part of becoming a vampire was knowing that we'd be together for centuries. I'd rather be executed for helping you than live without you."

"Don't say that!"

"It's true. I love you too much to watch them take you away so they can kill you. I won't do it. I won't let them take you."

"And I love you too much to let you risk your life for me."

"But that's just it, Parker. It's a risk if we run away, but it's a sure thing if we wait for Constance to take you. We have to at least try."

"Even if I found control in a few years, do you think the Assembly would forgive us? I'd have killed a lot of humans by that time, and you would be hiding a bloodthirsty vampire. They'd still execute both of us."

"Maybe not. I have to take a chance on that maybe."

"Ah, Holly, that's a hell of a chance."

"I can't give up on any hope we might have. Promise me we'll take that chance together."

"Okay ..." Parker was shaking his head again like he knew it was a bad idea. "But not until we've tried everything else."

"But, what if ..."

"Babe ..." Parker said as he cupped my cheek in his hand. "We've waited so long to be together." His thumb stroked my bottom lip. "Can we find another time to argue?"

As soon as he touched my lips I saw the love and longing in his eyes. Without me even telling them to, my hands started to roam. His sexy lips were right there almost touching mine.

I kissed that thumb that was still on my lips, and he moved over me as we met in an amazing, hot kiss. He strayed to the corner of my mouth, my cheek, my jaw, and finally my neck.

I could feel him inhale my scent. His teeth lightly grazed that sensitive spot below my ear, and I sighed.

"Bite me," I whispered and moved my head more to the side to give him better access.

Parker growled when I said that. A soft, pleasurable growl like lion cubs wrestling with each other, not the threatening growl of the dangerous predator that I'd heard the night he tried to attack Sarita.

He continued to kiss and nuzzle my neck before I felt that it was fangs stroking my skin. He used them to bite my earlobe without breaking the skin, he licked my neck, then he plunged those fangs into my vein.

It hurt for a second before he started to drink, then it felt amazing. A tingling warmth spread through my body. I felt like I must be glowing with the amazing sensation of Parker feeding at my neck.

He fed deeply and, each time he sucked, another wave of desire flowed through me. It was sexual desire, yet it was more. It was like I was sharing my very being with him and I never wanted him to stop.

I wanted him to devour me. I wanted the vampire blood in each of us to join and make us one. That blood, that essence that made us what we were, that kept us alive, merged the two of us into one.

He stopped. With his mouth still over the wound on my neck, Parker was still and breathing deeply like he'd run for miles. Then he licked the wounds and pulled his head back to look at me.

His eyes were bright with a look of utter amazement and his fangs were still distended through his gums.

"It felt like we shared our souls," he whispered.

"I felt the same thing." I took a gasping breath, realizing that I hadn't been breathing for quite some time.

"I love you so much, Holly."

He pulled our bodies even closer until we were on our sides, facing each other like that night my hunger wanted me to drain him. This time, my beast was quiet. All I felt was his strong body against mine as his hands roamed and caressed, and that was amazing. We kissed passionately and made love again. When we finally slept, we held each other like we'd never let go.

Chapter 17

The next thing I heard was a deep voice calling Parker's name from the other room, but he was still sound asleep. I flinched, thinking about getting out of bed and dressed, but there was no way I had time. The footsteps were at the bedroom door, and I was naked under Parker's down comforter. All I could do was stay where I was.

"Par ... Holly ...," TJ said as he entered the room. He looked away and held up a hand like it would block his view of us. "I'm sorry. I'll come back," and he started to back up.

"TJ, wait," I said. "Just give me a minute and I'll come out."

He nodded and closed the door behind him. Moving away from Parker to get up, I noticed him grinning.

I punched him in the shoulder. "You were pretending! Chicken!"

"I really was asleep until I heard your voice," he laughed.

"And left me to deal with TJ."

"You're so good at dealing with everyone." He smiled and grabbed my face and kissed me.

"If you know what's good for you, you'll go out there with me."

"I'd rather pretend to be asleep."

I tried to glare at him, but my lips couldn't help smiling a little.

"But I'll get dressed," he said.

We found TJ and Byron waiting for us in the living room. To my surprise, Byron glared at me. He only used that look when he was royally p.o.'d, and I wondered why he was so upset.

I knew TJ had to have told him that he found us in bed together, but was that really a big surprise? Everyone knew that we planned on moving in together as soon as Parker was a vampire and I wasn't a danger to him anymore.

"I thought you were here to guard him," Byron said looking directly at me.

Parker spoke up before I could answer. "Don't be mad at Holly. It was my fault."

Then Byron turned that glare toward Parker. "She was left with the responsibility to guard you, not entertain you."

"What's the big deal?" Parker's volume grew with his anger. "Neither of us left the suite, which is the idea. Right?"

"The idea," Byron wasn't shouting, but his voice and face were so intense, "is that you need to be watched and she slept."

"I don't believe it." Parker turned his head away from Byron like he was trying to control himself. Then he turned back. "You're still treating me like I'm a child. I'm not a child!" Now we were into real shouting.

"Oh, I know you're not a child. You're a predator! A bloodthirsty predator that can't be trusted alone for a moment." Byron didn't shout like Parker had, but his tone was even worse. It went beyond anger. It was accusatory and almost like he was disgusted.

TJ and I just stood there watching the two of them. What else could we do? He had that controlled, blank face that made him such a good guard, but my eyes were wide and my mouth hung open.

"I was right," Parker said quietly. "You know I can't control it and you think I should be killed like anyone else in bloodthirst. You're going to turn me over to Constance because, whether I'm your son or not, it's what you live by. A bloodthirsty vampire deserves to die! No exceptions for anyone. Right?"

Byron's face showed us several emotions as he stood there looking at Parker. From anger, he moved to fear, and finally to some kind of calmness, maybe resignation. Overall, though, he was conflicted. I don't think Byron knew for sure what he thought or felt.

That scared me. If he was confused, then part of him did think that Parker needed to die for being bloodthirsty. Part of Byron had not only lost hope, but had decided that killing Parker was the right thing to do.

Without saying another word, Byron turned and walked out of the suite.

Parker dropped his head and covered his eyes with one hand. I went to him and wrapped my arms around his waist.

"He's scared for you, Parker," TJ said.

"I need some time alone," Parker said quietly. "You two can hang out here if you want."

"Parker, let's talk about this," I said as I hugged him. "You shouldn't be alone."

"No, babe, I have to think. TJ, I'll call you when I'm hungry." Then he kissed my forehead, gently moved my arms away from him, and walked to the bedroom closing the door behind him.

TJ put his arm around my shoulders. "Go get ready for work," he said. "I'll give him a little time before I go in. I won't leave him alone for long." I realized TJ didn't give me any of the usual, "It'll be okay. Don't worry," type lines, because things might never be okay again.

"Call me if he asks for me?" I said without any emotion.

"Sure thing."

"TJ, I'm sorry. I didn't know Byron would be so mad."

"He's just worried. Too worried to know what he's doing."

* * *

Parker's mind was made up now. If Byron didn't believe in him, then there was no hope. No hope at all.

He went into his closet and grabbed his backpack. He wouldn't need much, just some extra clothes, so the small backpack would be fine. His GPS was in the car. Parker shook his head at himself, realizing he probably wouldn't need anything.

He put on jeans, a t-shirt, and hid a light jacket inside the closet with the backpack. That was it. He was ready, except for the necessity to feed.

Feeding would continue to be the problem. Once he was out of Rule the Night, he'd be on his own and the temptation to kill would be even greater. If he could avoid humans, he'd be okay until he got to Chicago.

Charles had to be in Chicago. He and Randall had talked over and over about their friends there. Friends that would hide him and do what they were told. So the only thing for Parker to do was get to Chicago to find Charles. Then he would kill him.

Parker stared across the room, knowing he had to face the hard part. He sat down at his computer and made a recording for Holly. It was all he could do not to cry as he spoke to her, but he couldn't leave her without any word. She had to know what he planned. He saved it to a data stick, then called TJ. He was hungry.

Parker let TJ tie him down, and Quinton brought him a human woman to feed from. She was delicious. Parker really tried to stop feeding when her heartbeat changed. He tried as hard as he could.

But that beast wouldn't let him stop. It wouldn't let him slow down. As he drank her blood, he sucked faster and faster, knowing that TJ and Quinton would be stopping him at any minute.

Once she was gone, he cried out a scream. He couldn't help it. His food was gone and he wanted it back. He wanted to stop feeding himself before TJ stepped in, but he couldn't. He wanted to drink her dry, but TJ and Quinton stopped him. He was so conflicted; he couldn't stand it anymore.

Quinton took the woman back to the bar while TJ gave Parker time to calm down before untying him. Then TJ would need to feed. Most nights, Byron would stay with Parker, but not tonight. Byron was too upset, and he'd let TJ and Q handle it.

"I'll be fine while you're gone," Parker said once he'd finally gotten himself back in control. "Go ahead and feed, and we'll watch some baseball when you come back."

"I won't be long," TJ answered.

The nightly feedings had been hard on Byron, TJ, and Quinton, but not just emotionally hard. It was forcing them to feed every night, which added to their own desire for bloodthirst.

Parker knew that no matter how strong a vampire was, bloodthirst was still deep inside them. The more they watched Parker's feedings and smelled that human blood, the more often they had to feed themselves, and that bloodthirsty beast kept pushing on their resolve. Another good reason to end this.

Parker had only a few minutes before TJ or Quinton would come back. Maybe both of them. If he didn't go now, he'd have to wait for the next evening because he had to get to Chicago before daylight.

He put on his jacket, grabbed his backpack, and threw the data stick on his bed. Holly'd find it there. She'd be hurt, but she'd eventually be okay. She'd eventually understand that he had to do this. He couldn't let her run away with him, so there wasn't any other choice.

He peeked down the hallway to make sure no one was within sight. The bar was filling fast with vampires and humans. Parker could smell them all. He held his nose so the smell of humans wasn't so tempting. Even though he'd just fed, the desire was there to run upstairs and attack someone.

From the hallway, to the family entrance, to his little green bug. He made it. He hadn't seen anyone and no one had seen him.

Parker pulled out of the garage as quickly as possible.

* * *

Charles stalked the street in one of the worst areas of Chicago. He knew the Assembly was looking for him, but had to take the chance. He needed to feed and the threat of the Assembly wouldn't stop him from enjoying the terror of his next victim.

This was the way they were meant to feed. Forget enthralling a human so they wouldn't feel the pain and taking little, polite sips of their blood. Forget wiping their memories so they'd never know they were attacked.

Vampires were meant to attack. Violent, bloody attacks. The humans should know the terror and feel the pain. His victims didn't need to have their memories wiped from their minds. His victims were dead.

He had finally healed from the injuries Byron had inflicted. The knee break had been the worst, almost as bad as the broken spine Holly'd given him, and running through that cemetery on a fractured knee hadn't helped. Now, though, he felt like his old self. Strolling the streets, hunting for a likely victim.

The whole fight with Byron had just made him more determined than ever to destroy him, and part of the plan had worked beautifully. Parker was bloodthirsty, Byron was protecting him, and Charles looked forward to when he heard that they had both been executed. Constance had sounded so shocked when he'd called her.

Sure, his plan to take a place on the Assembly had failed, but even that was being handled. Once Byron was gone, Charles would start gathering supporters again, and someday the vampire community could take the place it deserved in the world.

Someday, they'd all see that the human race was inferior and should be used as vampire food like humans used cows. Humans would someday live only to serve vampires and feed them. Vampires would rule, and humans would be nothing but the weak victims they were designed to be.

That was for the future. Right now, Charles's closest conspirator was Dawson, who was still with him only because he was weak and afraid. From that isolated cemetery in Columbus, he'd gotten through to Dawson first, and forced him to come get him.

Interesting that he couldn't find any of the others who'd been with him through the years. They'd all scattered to avoid being implicated, and Dawson was the only one foolish enough to stick around. Foolish enough to let Charles hide out in his basement.

This situation was only temporary. He had a plan and a friend on the Assembly. A friend that kept him informed, so he wouldn't need to hide for long.

He also had a friend who would start working on the next part. Donovan was almost as old as Charles and possibly even more bloodthirsty. He didn't have Charles's controlled determination or a vision of the long-term benefits of slow, careful strategy, but he'd be perfect for the next step.

There was no one better than Donavan to begin hunting in Columbus. The humans would know they should be afraid of the predator that stalked their streets, and bloodthirst would spread. To other cities, and to other states. Eventually, it would spread through the world whether the Assembly liked it or not. It was all going to come together very soon.

The scent of a human female wafted through the air and he spotted her coming toward him. She was young and very nicely dressed, probably a student at Lake Forest or one of the other snooty colleges around town. She should know better than to be alone on the streets so late at night. When she got close, he moved to his left to stop right in front of her almost demanding that she look in his eyes.

"Come with me," he said softly as he held out his hand to her.

She took his hand and followed. That brief glance of his eyes was all it took, and she was under his influence.

Charles led her to the back of a dark, dead-end alley and pressed her against the wall. He had to enchant her to keep her from screaming, even though he hated feeding without hearing her fear thrown out into the night, but he just couldn't take the chance that someone else would also hear her.

The fear was already in her eyes. He blocked her voice, but dropped the block of her emotions. The terror grew inside her, and Charles knew he'd enjoy this quite a bit.

Charles showed her his fangs as she struggled uselessly against him. She tried to break away, and he let her think for a second that she might make it. Then he effortlessly pulled her back as he laughed in her face.

She tried to scream, but Charles had made sure no sound came from her lips. As her mouth kept flying open in her silent screams, he plunged his fangs toward her and laughed again at the horror in her eyes.

Enough. He would have liked to keep up the games for a lot longer, but he knew Assembly spies could be anywhere. He just didn't have the time to truly enjoy her. He took both her hands, wrapped them behind her, and held them with one of his hands.

"You're going to be delicious," he snarled with his face just inches from hers. "I will enjoy this a great deal."

His fist wrapped around the back of her head, grasping her hair. He pulled her head back without taking his eyes off hers. Then he bit.

She struggled, fought against his body, tried to free her hands as if she could get away from him. He would have laughed if the taste of her blood hadn't been so remarkable. She was so young, and her blood was so clean and healthy.

For a few seconds he considered letting her live and keeping her so he could feed from her again, thinking that she could be an excellent replacement for Clair. But, no. He didn't have anywhere to keep her, and couldn't afford to let himself get lost in her taste.

He sucked harder at her vein and listened to her heart slowing. It wouldn't be long. All her struggles were soon over and she slumped against the wall, only held in a standing position by his strong body and his hand in her hair.

Then her heart stopped.

Charles sucked deeply one more time and lifted his head from her neck.

"Yes," he whispered, "it would have been nice to have kept you."

Then he stepped back watching her lifeless body slump to the filthy floor of the alley. He picked her up and placed her in a half-empty dumpster. He didn't really care if she was found or not. No one would ever trace her to him, and the humans could just continue to wonder what happened to her blood.

He felt strong, powerful, and ready to take on the world as he strolled back toward his little basement prison. He wouldn't be in that basement for long. No, not for long at all. Plans were already coming together.

Dawson's house wasn't empty as he assumed it would be. Lights were on in the huge, old house showing the presence of several vampires. Charles hoped it would be good news.

Chapter 18

Parker drove as fast as he could. While still on the city streets, he could smell the humans around him and he wanted them. It was early evening and a lot of people were out, but, thankfully, their scent wafting into the car was faint and distant. That's the only thing that saved them.

Going 70 MPH down the country road that led to the freeway, the surrounding humans were finally far enough away that there was no trace of them. No longer distracted by humans, he began to keep his eyes open for cops.

All he needed was to be stopped for speeding. That would be a traffic stop that the cop wouldn't survive. Parker hadn't been able to keep it together when they brought Chris in. A stranger standing outside his driver-side window? No way would he be able to resist that.

Besides, he didn't have time to be distracted by humans. There was no doubt that Byron and the guards would be out looking for him as soon as they discovered he was gone, and that wouldn't take long. TJ would be heading back to Parker's room from feeding any minute now, and they would start looking.

Hopefully, they'd think he was headed for Columbus and not realize he'd be traveling northwest to Chicago. They had no clue that Charles still had connections in Chicago and planned to go back there after the whole business at the mausoleum.

Parker'd overheard several discussions while being held prisoner and hadn't told anyone. Actually, it just didn't seem important and he'd practically forgotten about it until recently. After Constance's visit, Parker spent a lot of time thinking through where Charles could be and that led him to finally remember what he'd overheard.

He had to be back in Chicago by now, and someone at Nibble would know where. The Assembly had taken over the sanctuary, but some of those working with Charles would still be keeping an eye on the place.

All Parker would have to do is ask around because Charles would want Parker back. He'd love to have another chance to kill Parker, and that's just what Parker would give him. At least that's what Charles would think. Parker's plan, though, was to shoot him on sight.

It was the story of what Chris had accomplished at that place in Columbus that had given Parker his inspiration. Man to man, Parker didn't have a chance against Charles. But with the gun? He could take Charles down.

Parker finally got to the outskirts of Chicago at about 1:00 a.m. He remembered very well the way to Nibble. He also remembered how scared he was that night he thought Holly wouldn't forgive him for purposely cutting himself to get her to feed from him. Man, how had he ever thought that was a good idea?

Looking back, he knew everything was his fault. If he hadn't cut himself, then she never would have met Charles, and the rest of this whole mess wouldn't have happened.

Adelle High School graduation was next week, and he and Holly would be looking forward to starting their lives together. Byron would be changing him, and everything would be great!

If only he hadn't been so selfish. If only he'd had some patience. Yeah. If only.

But through it all, somehow, Holly still loved him. She'd come to him without a moment's hesitation or second thought. Making love to her had been even more incredible than anything he'd fantasized about.

Maybe he shouldn't have had sex with Holly when he'd been thinking about leaving, but he couldn't resist her. Her plans to run away with him settled everything in his mind. That's what made him determined to go immediately.

There was no way Parker could let Holly throw her life away for him. She'd have a chance now to make choices for herself. She'd have the opportunity to find someone else. Someone who was strong enough to control their instincts and make a life with her. She'd be happy again.

It would take awhile, probably. Holly would hold on to her love for him long after he died, Parker was sure of that. But, eventually, she'd move on. She needed to move on.

Those thoughts brought a tear to Parker's eyes. He loved her with all his heart and soul, and he knew she loved him. He also knew that he would never be able to control his bloodthirst. It was just wishful thinking that they could run away and hide together.

He forced himself to stop thinking about Holly. Holly was taken care of, and making sure Charles paid for what he'd done was all Parker had time to worry about now.

Parker slowed down as he passed through the streets leading to Nibble. It may be the middle of the night, but there were still too many humans around. He had to do something to keep their smell away from him, or he'd never get the chance to find Charles.

He reached across the passenger seat to the little first aid kit that Crystal had put in his glove compartment when he first got the car. Wadding up a piece of gauze, he stuffed it into his right nostril. Then he stuffed one into the left.

He pushed them back as far as he could so they were out of sight. It helped, but breathing through his mouth still let some of the human scent through, so he just stopped breathing. Hopefully, a periodic, small breath wouldn't tempt him.

Parker pulled to the curb down the street from Nibble. He'd be ready as soon as the place closed at 2:30 and the human customers were gone. Then he could go in and start asking for Charles. Start to offer himself to Charles. Otherwise, there was nothing to do. There was no Plan B.

Parker hadn't thought that blocking the scent of humans also meant he couldn't smell vampires. Not even the two large males that were approaching from behind him and getting closer to his car. Parker was concentrating on the door into Nibble, and he had no clue the vampires were right next to him.

The driver's door suddenly flew open, and Parker was dragged from his seat. He was gagged, blindfolded and tied up before he knew what was happening. Then he was carried a short distance, and thrown into what must have been a van because it started up and drove away.

It all happened so fast, and Parker didn't have much of a chance fighting against the two vampires that grabbed him. Once he was settled in the back of the van, though, he realized this might be just what he needed. This might be the Plan B that Parker couldn't have arranged.

These guys would take him to Charles. They must have been on patrol around Nibble, and spotted him as he parked the bug. The happy coincidence of them being on patrol just as Parker got there was probably making them feel like they'd accidentally caught the one thing Charles wanted most.

It was making Parker think the same. He'd lucked into being captured and taken to Charles. The thing *he* wanted most.

He still had the gun right there in his holster, and everything would go as planned. As soon as he was in front of Charles, he'd pull the gun and shoot right through his brain.

What would happen next? Parker had no doubt that Charles's guards would jump him. He'd try to shoot them, too, but there might be too many of them. Or, he could miss, and they'd overpower him. They'd kill him immediately if they got their hands on him.

Didn't matter. Parker knew that, one way or another, he'd be dead soon. Either Charles's guards would kill him, or he'd call Constance to come and get him.

Even with the thought of dying in his head, Parker couldn't help smiling a little as he lay there in the back of that van. Charles's guys were doing exactly what Parker wanted.

* * *

I saw Byron coming across the bar with a look on his face that I didn't like at all. He looked like he was ready to kill someone and was headed straight for me. He couldn't still be that mad about me sleeping with Parker instead of guarding him, could he? No, this had to be something else. Something was really wrong.

"Where is Parker?" he growled as he stepped behind the bar and got right in front of me.

I almost dropped the glass of club soda I was handing to a waitress. Parker missing? This was bad.

"Isn't he in his room?" I asked. What a dumb question. His room is where he was supposed to be. Byron wouldn't have asked if Parker'd been where he was supposed to be.

Byron's nostrils flared with anger. "Obviously not. Where did he go?"

229

"I don't know. Have you looked everywhere?"

"Holly, he must have confided in you. What is he doing?"

"I don't know!" I yelled and noticed several customers glancing at us.

Byron just glared. Was he listening? I was ready to scream because now I was on the edge of panic. Parker missing? Where could he be? God, he could be out on the streets killing someone.

TJ came up behind Byron. "Byron," he said holding out a data stick to him. I could see it had my name on it.

"What's that?" I asked.

Byron glared at me. "Come on," he growled and grabbed my upper arm to lead me toward his office.

"It was in the middle of Parker's bed," TJ said as we marched across the bar. "He obviously wanted us to find it."

Byron didn't say anything. He just steamed ahead and never let go of my arm. All I could think about was what Parker might have done. Had he left without me? How could he?

There'd be no one to hide him, no one to protect him. Where could he go to sleep and avoid the sun all day? I was trembling with worry and sure Byron could feel it through his hand.

Bryon took the data stick from TJ and slipped it into his computer's USB port. No one said anything as it loaded, but I guess there really wasn't anything to say.

Parker appeared in front of us sitting at his computer. He looked so sad, yet determined. Then he started talking.

"Holly, you're not going to like this, but I had to leave on my own. I can't let you take the risk of being found with me. I love you too much for that.

"We have to face that I'm not going to be able to control this. Byron's right. I'm not going to get better, and the Assembly is going to have to come back to get me. And they should.

"I don't want to kill, but I can't stop it. I'm afraid it's getting worse, and I need to be turned over to them. I can't let Byron be involved in that. He probably thinks it's his duty or something, but it would destroy him. I can't let him do it."

Parker stopped there for a few seconds and looked away from the camera. He looked like he was on the verge of crying and was trying really hard not to. After a minute, he turned back to the camera.

"I have an idea where Charles might be. I'm going to kill him and turn myself in to the Assembly. Tell Byron not to bother looking for me 'cause it could all be over by morning. Charles is probably dying to get me back, so it shouldn't take long at all for me to get to him."

He paused again looking like he was thinking about what he wanted to say next.

"Holly, I want you to go on with your life. I want you to find someone else and be happy with him. That may seem hard right now, but eventually you'll find someone else to love. You'll be happy. Please, be happy so I know you're okay."

Another pause. He swallowed like it was getting harder for him not to break down and cry.

"I think God will let me into Heaven, don't you? I think He knows I didn't want to kill those women. I'll be with my parents, so you don't have to worry about me. But I'll be watching out for you. I'll always watch out for you. I love you."

Parker turned away from the webcam and turned it off.

I had started crying the moment I saw him on the screen, but, by the end, I was sobbing and dropped to the floor on my knees. Byron threw his chair back and knelt down beside me.

I saw the tears rolling down his cheeks when I looked up at him. All I could do was throw my arms around him and cry on his chest. He held me and we cried.

I'd forgotten about TJ until I realized his hand was on the back of my head and he was stroking my hair. I looked up. His eyes were closed, and he looked devastated, too.

"Sir," TJ said with his gruff, military voice. "I'm going after him."

"Where?" Byron asked.

"Columbus or Chicago are the best bets. I can't do nothing."

"Take whoever else you need."

TJ left and I turned from Byron's chest to watch him go. I didn't have much hope they'd find Parker, but, God, I hoped they did.

"I'm sorry I suspected you," Byron said quietly.

"I told him I wanted the two of us to run away together. I planned on hiding until he could control his bloodthirst no matter how long it took."

"He couldn't let you do that."

"We could have been together."

"I know."

He hadn't let go of me, and I dropped my head back to his shoulder.

"I'm going to my room," I said quietly, moving away from him, and getting up off the floor. "Can I have that?"

He took the data stick from the computer and handed it to me. "I'll send Crystal so you're not alone," he said quietly.

"No. I want to be alone for a while."

"How about Chris?"

"Really," I shook my head. "I'll be okay."

I walked out and down to my room like some kind of zombie. I passed several people in the hallway and more on the stairs, but I have no idea who they were. I was so numb I couldn't even think.

Slipping off my shoes, I crawled onto the bed and lay on my back staring up at the ceiling. I wasn't crying. I wasn't thinking. Except for my faint heartbeat, I could have been dead. I felt dead.

Parker was gone.

Forever.

ABOUT THE AUTHOR

Ellen Fritz is a retired teacher and high school counselor. Over the years of teaching reading and English to students in grades seven through twelve before be-coming a counselor, she had the great opportunity to discuss numerous favorite books with students and also took their recommendations for her own reading.

She finally found herself with the time to give life to the stories that have always been patiently waiting in her head for an audience. Ellen wrote <u>Mira</u> to appeal to those middle grade/teen readers that she found so inspiring through her career as an educator.

"I didn't start writing seriously until I retired and found myself with the time to spend a whole day in front of the computer. The ideas had been in my head for many years, but were undeveloped and unexplored. One day, several months after my teaching/ counseling career ended, I sat down and started.

Some days, the ideas, dialog, and characters flow from my brain and I can barely type fast enough. Other days, I have to walk away, occupy my mind with something else, and hash through what might happen, what might be said. But both days are valuable.

While waiting for a publisher to accept my first book, I discovered that rejections were okay. While I want young people to read and enjoy my books, I realized that the writing was more for me. It's a joy to develop the characters and situations, and I can't foresee a time when I'll be ready for it to end."

Tell-Tale Publishing would like to thank you for your purchase. If you would like to read more from this or other fine TT authors, please visit our website:

http://www.tell-talepublushing.com

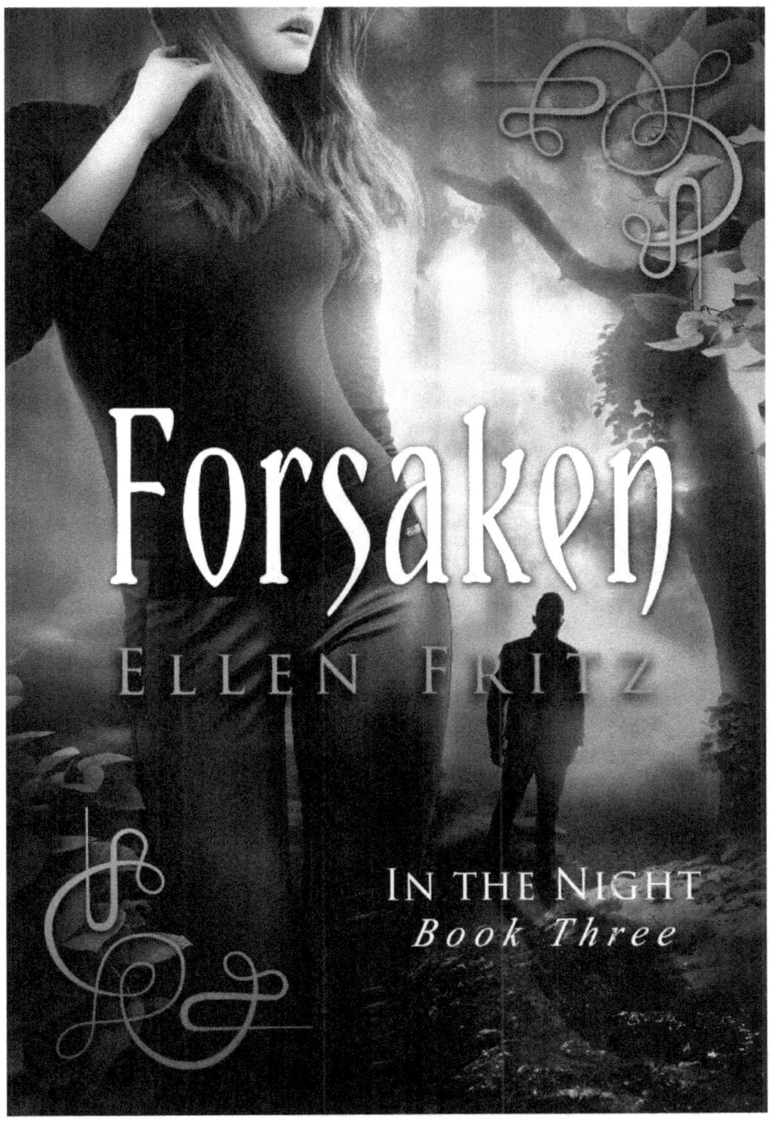

Free Sneak Peek at Book Three from the In the Night Series!

Chapter 1

Someone was shaking me.

"Holly. Wake up, Holly."

I slowly opened my eyes from a very sound sleep to see Chris leaning over me with his hand on my shoulder. *Parker's dead!* I thought even before I'd had time to move.

"Parker?" I asked. I didn't want him to say it. *Please don't say it.*

"No! We haven't heard anything about Parker," Chris said shaking his head vigorously. Then he held still and looked serious. "It's Mom and Dad."

"What?" I was still waking up and not thinking clearly with the dread of hearing about Parker in my head. What could Chris be trying to tell me?

"There was an accident last night." He hesitated like he was trying to choose the right words. "They're dead, Holly," he practically whispered. "They were killed in the accident."

I realized then why Chris looked the way he did. His eyes were puffy and red, he was sniffing, and his lip quivered a little when he wasn't speaking.

"They're dead?" My brain was empty except for the need to repeat what I'd just heard. Could I have heard him right?

"The police called me this morning. I guess Mom got out of jail yesterday, and they went out last night."

"They were drunk," I sighed. I wasn't asking. I knew.

"Yeah."

"Uncle Steve driving?" Mom and Dad didn't have a car anymore, but Uncle Steve did. He was still living with them since Chris and I left, so it just made sense that he'd be driving.

"Uncle Steve told the cops that Dad said he was okay to drive, so he was driving Uncle Steve's car. He plowed into a tree. Uncle Steve was passed out in the back seat. He doesn't remember anything, and wasn't hardly hurt. Just scrapes and bruises."

"When did they call?"

"About 7:00. Someone found the car this morning along that road by the river. They didn't have seatbelts on. Steve was still passed out in the back, and they took him to the hospital and everything to have him checked out. The whole thing's a mess," Chris was shaking his head like he couldn't get a handle on everything the cops told him. "I just keep thinking that I'm glad he didn't hit another car and kill someone else."

That's when I started crying because I knew it was real. Neither Mom nor Dad usually drove when they were drinking. Drunk driving was Uncle Steve's specialty. Chips was close enough to easily walk home, and a lot of the time they drank at home anyway. I was always thankful for that because, that way, neither of them would kill someone else. But now, Dad had killed himself and Mom.

Chris hugged me and we just held each other for a few minutes, both of us crying.

"I can't believe it," I blubbered, looking up at Chris. "I've meant to go see them, but … you know. I never knew what to say, and Uncle Steve was always there. I … I just can't believe it."

"I have to go talk to the funeral home in about an hour and arrange things."

"What? God, I forgot about all that. Can I help you? I mean, can you do it at night?"

"I already asked them," Chris said shaking his head. "I wanted you to go, too."

"I don't want you to have to do this all by yourself," I practically whined.

"I called Aunt Sarah." That surprised me. Uncle Steve's wife, in the process of becoming ex-wife, was not a favorite person to either one of us. "The cops already called her about Uncle Steve, so I figured she was the easiest, and he's still sleeping it off, so he won't be there. It won't be so bad."

"Oh Chris, I'm sorry," I said through a sob. I hated that he'd have to handle everything alone. My next thought made my voice stronger. "But don't let her think she's running the show. Remember how she got Grandma's funeral all out of control?"

"I sure do, but not this time," Chris said with determination. "I was thinking about something really simple. No calling hours. Just a simple prayer at the cemetery, if that's okay with you."

"Sure, that's fine with me, but it's what you want that counts. I can't be there, so make it what you want."

"Okay," he nodded. "But, you know, any funeral is really expensive, and, hell, this is *two*. I have some money saved, but I know it's not enough. Do you have any?"

"Sure. Most of my salary's still in the bank. But don't worry about the cost. Byron will loan us whatever we need until we sell the house. Unless you want the house?"

"Oh, hell no! And I don't think I want anything that's in it."

"Me neither."

"I'd better go. I'm meeting Aunt Sarah at the funeral home. I told the hospital Carson-Grant over on Pine Street. That okay?"

"That's fine."

Tears started pooling in Chris's eyes again. "I don't want to do this, Holly. Even if you were there ... I just don't know what to do."

"I know." I hugged him again. "I wish I could help you. Did Lorna have any advice to give you?"

"She didn't hear the phone, and I didn't wake her up. Nobody knows, but you."

"They'll want to know. Come get me when you get back, and we'll tell them together."

"I don't want to wake you up again."

"You won't. I'll be thinking about you, not sleeping."

"I'm sorry, Holly. I didn't want to wake you up to tell you all this. It's just ... hell, I'm sorry."

"Don't say that. I'm sorry you have to handle everything alone. Just ..." I shook my head, not knowing for sure what I wanted to say. "Just stay strong with Aunt Sarah, and we'll talk when you get back." I reached up to touch the side of his face.

Chris hugged me again and left for the funeral home. I watched him walk out the door and thought about him being the only family I had left. And if Parker didn't come back ... No. I couldn't think about that now.

As a young vampire, I'd someday have to face the death of every human I knew, but I really didn't think it'd be this soon. Then I started thinking about Mom and Dad. Dead. It was so unreal.

How long had it been since I'd seen them? I still saw them like they were when I left that night. I couldn't ever really see Mom in jail like Chris said she was. So unreal.

We'd have to get rid of all their stuff and sell the house. How do you do all that? And I was sure the house was a complete

mess. I was the only one who ever cleaned the last few years and I
hadn't been there since last fall. Where would we start?

Two hours later, I still sat there thinking all my scattered
thoughts, but Chris was back. "How was it?" I asked without even
saying hello.

"Not bad," he answered, trying to smile a little. "The
funeral director was cool. He explained everything. I had to tell
Aunt Sarah that you and I'd decided how we wanted it, and he
figured out really quick that I was making the decisions. So he
pretty much ignored her and talked to me."

"That's good."

"We'll meet the hearse at the cemetery the day after
tomorrow, one of the funeral home guys will say a little prayer,
and that'll be it."

"Good."

"The caskets, burial plots, all that stuff really costs a lot,
though. It'll be close to $10,000 for the two of them. And I didn't
even pick out the fancy caskets. Are you sure Byron will give us a
loan?"

"Of course he will. I'll bet he'll want to pay for it, but
we'll pay him back as soon as the house sells. I think the two of us
need to pay for it."

"Oh, yeah. We do."

"Thank you, Chris. I'm really proud of you for handling all
this."

"Thanks. I guess you do what you have to, you know?"

I smiled at him and kissed his cheek. "Let's go tell Lorna
and Byron. We'll let them tell the rest."

"Should we wake them?"

"They'll want us to," I nodded

We decided to take Lorna with us to tell Byron because we only wanted to tell the story once. I couldn't face going through the whole thing multiple times, and I was sure Chris had had enough talking about Mom and Dad with Aunt Sarah and the funeral directors.

So we woke up Lorna and asked her to go to Byron with us. She was worried, and kept asking us questions from the bathroom while she got dressed.

"It's not about Parker, or anything, but it's bad news," Chris told her. "We just don't want to go through it a bunch of times."

"Are you two okay?" she asked, looking worried.

"We're fine," I said. We were fine, but I think both of us were pretty numb. I just couldn't get it to sink in and be real. Chris was probably doing better than me since he talked to the funeral home, but I didn't really know if he was, or not.

Byron and Crystal, like Lorna, were sleeping soundly when we woke them. It was about noon, the middle of the night for vampires, but we knew they'd never forgive us if we let them sleep. Again, we had to quickly tell them that it wasn't about Parker. He was constantly on everyone's mind.

They put on robes, and we all sat in Byron's living room to talk. I could feel the tension as we gathered. They knew it wasn't about Parker, but they all wondered why on Earth we would wake them like we did.

"Mom and Dad were killed last night in a car accident," Chris started without any intro. But what could you say? Except the blunt, horrible truth.

Tears came to my eyes immediately. I knew that telling other people would start to make it real, but I guess that's the way it should be. It was real.

Everyone knows it will be hard to face the death of family and friends, but I guess no one really knows which parts will be the worst. I was finding out that telling other people that needed to be told could be pretty bad.

Byron held us both, Lorna and Crystal cried, I cried, Chris cried. It was everything anyone would expect from telling someone both of your parents had just died. Horrible, but wonderful that our friends cared so much for us.

Byron asked all the how, when, where questions and praised Chris for handling all the details himself. Lorna said he should have woken her up, and he said he needed to tell me first and how he wished she could have helped with the funeral home. Crystal just told us how sorry she was and held me.

Eventually, we got to the money part. Byron said he'd pay for everything, and we said we only needed a loan. He wanted us to keep all the money from the sale of the house, and we said that we felt we needed to pay for the funeral ourselves.

"Byron," I finally said. "I think we need to pay you back so it's real. It hasn't sunk in, and I think it will if we handle stuff ourselves. We have to pay you back."

"Okay," he finally relented, "but I'll call my lawyer, Clyde Reynolds. He'll handle everything, and I have him on retainer, so there'll be no extra cost. I haven't needed him for quite a while, so he can earn what I've already paid him."

"We need a lawyer?" I asked.

"Well, there's inheritance tax, your father probably had life insurance at work, all the bills from the rescue, and do you know if the house still has a mortgage?"

"Grandma left the house to them. It's paid for."

"Good, that makes things a little easier. You won't have to be in a hurry to dispose of it."

"We talked about getting rid of it right away," I answered.

"You shouldn't be in a hurry," he said gently. "It takes time to let everything settle in and make sure you're doing the best thing for both of you."

"What do you think, Chris?"

"Maybe we should go over there after the funeral and look around. Then we can talk about it some more."

"That's a good idea," Byron said. "And you'll need Clyde to make sure everything's squared away before you make any decisions."

By the time we left Byron and Crystal, it was 2:00 in the afternoon. We all agreed to try to get some more sleep, but Chris and Lorna didn't want to leave me alone. They sat in my room while I crawled in bed, and we talked quietly.

I know they were both trying to get my mind on something else so I'd sleep. The surprising thing was that it worked. I felt myself drifting away as Lorna was quietly talking about when she lived in Paris.

I guess they left after I was asleep, because the next thing I knew I was waking up and it was almost 5:00.

That night Chris and I both worked because we had to do something. Byron said we could take the time off to do whatever we wanted, but we both wanted to work. The only thing there was to do was to go over to Mom and Dad's house, but we couldn't face that until after the funeral.

The day of the funeral came, and I didn't want to let go of Chris to go bury our parents without me. I wanted more than anything to be able to walk into that cemetery with him and hold his hand while the caskets were lowered into the graves, but that wasn't an option for me anymore.

"Don't let Uncle Steve and Aunt Sarah give you any kind of shit," I said. "You know they'll both try something. Stay strong and just do what *you* want."

"I will, little sis. And I'll feel you beside me the whole time."

"I'll be there," I said through my tears.

While Chris was gone, I paced around my room. The TV was on, but I didn't pay any attention to it. Crystal, Lorna, and Byron all came to be with me during the time of the funeral, even though they should have been sleeping.

We'd asked the three of them to tell everyone else what had happened. All the employees stopped to offer me a few words, but the hardest person to see was Sarita.

She stayed with me for about a half hour, even though she'd been really sick lately, and looked to me like she was getting older by the day. Dr. Jamison said she had the beginnings of Alzheimer's, but it seemed to me she was beyond the beginnings.

She remembered those she had known for a long time, but often forgot all kinds of things, even stuff that she knew an hour before. Byron had hired a vampire to help Anna with the cleaning, because we were just too busy anymore for one person to handle it. Sometimes, though, Sarita still went up and cleaned something just because it was what she had done for so many years.

Besides the worry over Sarita's health, the hardest thing was when she talked about Parker. She remembered everything from when he was a little boy and when he was a teenager, but she never remembered that he was missing.

We'd told her the truth about Charles taking him and about him running away, but she acted like none of it ever happened. She talked about Parker like she'd just seen him in the kitchen, or on his computer that day. He'd been gone several days by this time.

It broke my heart.

"Are you still sweet on Parker?" she asked as we sat on my bed talking to Byron, Crystal, and Lorna."

"Sure am," I answered.

"I knew all along you two liked each other. Is he at school?"

"I guess."

We decided there was no sense in telling her over and over that Parker was gone. It was like her brain refused to accept it. We just let her believe what made her happy.

Byron sighed deeply and closed his eyes while he listened to us talking. He knew it wouldn't be much longer before she needed round-the-clock care, but he'd hire whoever he had to, to help her. Dr. Jamison was already searching the country for a live-in nurse that knew about vampires. Not any easy person to find.

Parker and Sarita were Byron's adopted children, and he was losing both of them. He couldn't do anything about Sarita getting old and sick since she chose not to be a vampire. But there had to be something he could do to find Parker. I didn't see how he could give up on that.

Chris finally came back and said everything had gone fine at the funeral. A lot of the guys Dad had worked with showed up, and even some friends Mom and Dad had gone out drinking with. He thought half the regulars from Chips were there.

While they were waiting for the funeral to start, Uncle Steve had brought up who was going to pay for his car which was totaled in the accident. I would have slugged him if I'd been there.

"I told him that Dad didn't have a car, so he didn't have any insurance," Chris said. "I said that he'd have to sue us, but since he handed the keys to a man obviously too drunk to drive, he probably wouldn't get very far."

"Good for you, Chris," I said. "He's not getting a penny of our money."

"I guess I should tell your lawyer about that when we talk?" Chris asked Byron.

"Definitely," Byron answered. "But, you're right. He won't get anything."

We sat in Byron's suite the rest of the day after getting Sarita back to her room to rest. She was so tired all the time anymore. Besides, she kept forgetting that we'd just buried our parents and kept talking about Parker. I could hardly stand it much more, even though I loved Sarita and knew she meant well.

Chris and I went to work that night, but Byron came to get us about 10:00.

"We're going for a walk," he said to Chris and me.

"I'm good," Chris said. "You two go ahead."

"No, you're coming, too," Byron said. "Crystal and Luke can handle the bar."

We walked through the warm night, and I immediately felt a little better. A little more normal. I was in the middle with my arm through Byron's elbow and Chris holding my other hand. It felt good to have that support, but I put my arm around Chris's waist so he could reach around my shoulders. Chris needed the support as much as I did. Maybe more since there was so much he had to handle himself.

We walked silently, and I wasn't paying any attention to where we were heading, but, before I knew it, we were at the gates to the cemetery. I figured out what Byron was up to, but wasn't sure I wanted to go to the graves. I went anyway.

The cemetery workers had covered the graves with some kind of fake grass and a few bouquets of flowers that people had sent. I was glad the graves weren't bare dirt.

"It's nice here," I said as Chris and I stood there staring down at the graves and still holding each other.

"I didn't want them out by the road. It cost a little more back here, but I picked these anyway."

"Good. I'm glad you did. I'm so sorry you had to do everything on your own." Tears were slipping silently down my checks.

"I know. But it was okay."

"I can't believe Uncle Steve and Aunt Sarah didn't give you any trouble except for the car."

Chris sighed. "I wasn't going to tell you, but I guess you should know."

"What?"

"Aunt Sarah had this guy come with doves that he was going to let loose to symbolize their souls flying up to Heaven."

"You're kidding? They didn't have any religion. They wouldn't have wanted that." The tears had stopped immediately as my anger at Steve and Sarah flared.

"I kicked him out, and she was pissed off during the whole thing. Then, after the funeral, both of them started going on about where you were."

"Damn. What did they say?"

"You know," he shrugged. "Shit like the least a daughter could do was come to the funeral. I lost it and told them they needed to stay out of our lives. Uncle Steve started arguing, and I told him to go to hell."

"Good for you."

"I just wanted it to be peaceful, you know? And they had to start shit."

"Nothing is ever peaceful with Uncle Steve and Aunt Sarah involved."

He squeezed my shoulders a little and we stood there. Looking at those graves, it was finally becoming real. Mom and Dad were dead. I'd never see them again.

"Why am I so sad," I said through eyes that were tearing up again, "when I spent most of my life hating them?"

"You hated the stuff they did, and what they let drinking do to them, but they were still our parents. When we were little, we had some good times, didn't we?"

"Yeah, we did. I remember. I always hoped they'd somehow quit drinking and we'd get back to those days. I guess it's sad that that hope is gone now. Drinking actually killed them."

"Yeah, it did. You ready to go? We could stay longer if you want."

"No, I'm ready. What about tombstones? Are they expensive? How do we get them?"

"I don't know. We'll ask Byron if he knows."

I'd forgotten about Byron while we stood talking, but expected to see him when I turned around. He wasn't there. Looking across all the tombstones, I spotted him waiting at the gate. He'd given us private time and moved away to where even his vampire ears wouldn't hear what we had to say to each other.

On the silent walk back to Rule the Night, I started to think about how good this vampire family was to us. Who would have thought that vampires would be so nice? Why couldn't our real family have been so supportive and caring? I knew the answer to that. Alcohol.

Mom and Dad really were good people at heart, but they'd been drinking too much since they were teenagers. Even when we were little, and they were sober most days, getting drunk occupied too much of their time.

I wondered how different our lives would have been if Mom and Dad hadn't started drinking. Who knew? My childhood was what it was, and I couldn't change the past. All I could do was move on from it. My biggest worry was always that they'd hurt themselves or someone else when they were drunk. At least I didn't have to worry about that anymore.

Mostly, though, I couldn't stop thinking that I just couldn't take one more thing. Parker gone, and maybe dead, because he'd been purposefully turned into a bloodthirsty vampire by Charles, the most hateful, evil vampire I could imagine.

Byron as hurt and terrified as I was, living through each day, waiting to hear what had happened to Parker. He'd adopted Parker only ten years before, but couldn't have loved him anymore if he'd been his natural son. Everyone at Rule the Night loved Parker.

Now, my parents. Thank God I had Chris. He'd turned out to be everything that I ever hoped a big brother could be. But even though I had Chris, I knew that I wouldn't be able to handle one more thing.

www.ingramcontent.com/pod-product-compliance
Lightning Source LLC
Chambersburg PA
CBHW071143180726
48291CB00007B/2320